HEATHER

Also by Mollie Schmidt

Willem of Holland

Levi

HEATHER

Mollie Schmidt

iUniverse, Inc.
Bloomington

Heather

This is a work of fiction. All of the characters, names, incidents, organizations, and dialogue in this novel are either the products of the author's imagination or are used fictitiously.

iUniverse books may be ordered through booksellers or by contacting:

iUniverse
1663 Liberty Drive
Bloomington, IN 47403
www.iuniverse.com
1-800-Authors (1-800-288-4677)

ISBN: 978-1-4759-2171-7 (sc)
ISBN: 978-1-4759-2172-4 (hc)
ISBN: 978-1-4759-2173-1 (e)

Library of Congress Control Number: 2012907808

Printed in the United States of America

iUniverse rev. date: 5/10/2012

For Rosalie

To The Reader

WELCOME TO THE LAND of northern Maine, where porcupines eat the tires off your car, kids ride downhill on jumpbumpers, and, yes, moose really do climb on cars! Heather and her two friends work hard training their horses for trails, dressage, and team-penning, not always meeting with success, but hoping to win their laurels as team-penning champs.

Heather's brother, Ben, has a different task: to deal with a heart condition and still be able to ski, carry wood and hold an after-school job. Heather and Ben enjoy the special seasonal treats that Maine offers: a Turkey Trot with a Poker Trail, a sleigh ride behind a Clydesdale, and an equine fair.

The Maine winter plays a role in this exciting story about hardihood and courage and love for horses. And a pot-bellied pig!

CHAPTER ONE

L ATE ON A NOVEMBER night in northern Maine, the snow
began to fall. Silent as the deer huddled in the woods, it filled
the nooks between the rocks and trees, covered the leaves and
pine needles that lay on the ground, and weighted branches until
they hung low. Bushes became ghostly white shapes looming in
the dark forest.

Heather woke at five as usual. She stretched out in bed,
yawning. The windowpanes of her room were black before
sunrise, but she could see something light moving behind them.
She peered out through the flakes and whistled.

"Maybe a foot of snow already! No school!"

She watched the falling flakes for a moment, trying to guess
how deep the snow lay on the ground. It looked like a blizzard,
a white-out, which meant she couldn't see through it.

Her Friesian horse, Hendrik was seven months old. He had
never seen snow. It would be fun to show him this cold, soft
stuff. Hendrik had grown a good, thick coat for the Maine
winter. He would love snow!

Heather thought about the chores she would have lots of
time to do with no school. The first one was breakfast. She
sighed, remembering the big hearty breakfasts her mother used

to make – pancakes with maple, biscuits, baked French toast with eggs… Well, it was her job now.

She went downstairs and used a hook to lift one of the plates in the kitchen stove. There were embers still glowing inside, so she added kindling sticks and small sticks of wood. Soon she was stirring a pot of oatmeal. She was dressed warmly in a turtleneck sweater and jeans that were snug over her long winter underwear. Her brother, Ben, came running into the kitchen.

"Oh, boy! School's closed for sure!"

She looked at his pajamas and bare feet. "Go back up and get your clothes on," she ordered. "We've got chores, whether there's school or not. Dad's out plowing already!"

Heather was seventeen. In the absence of their mother, who had died of cancer two years before, she ran the house—and much of the horse farm, too. It was situated in the outskirts of China, Maine, with fields in a clearing near woods with several trails for horseback riding. Their father, Alan Hobbes, was a farm machinery salesman, whose work often took him to other states. When he was away, Heather did the plowing.

Ben, who was fourteen, generally did what Heather said. Besides, his feet were cold. He sprinted up the stairs to get his blood going.

"Not so fast!" Heather called. She had to supervise Ben sometimes when he rushed around. His heart wasn't in the left side of his chest, like most people's, but in the center. He was born that way. He needed a device called a "pacemaker" for his heart, but the doctor was waiting for him to be big enough for it. Heather worried sometimes that Ben was too active.

Most of the time, Ben didn't think about his heart. He ran around the farm, climbing fences and trees, as well as doing chores. He helped exercise the horses, played baseball at school, and enjoyed skiing. But he did get tired sometimes.

Now he dressed, planning to wax his skis, so he could take the trail through the woods that edged the paddock. *I remember where my skis are—they're hung on the wall in the stable along with the poles—I'll wax "em as soon as I get the wood in.* Whistling, he trotted down the stairs and headed toward the kitchen for breakfast. Heather gave him a steaming bowl of oatmeal with brown sugar and walnuts. He settled in at the old wooden table with the tin top.

There was a scratching at the door. Pinky Pie!

"He's hungry," Heather said.

Ben got out of his seat to let the potbellied pig in from the mudroom where he was bedded down at night. Pinky Pie was still quite small at one year. He rooted around the legs of the kitchen chairs, searching for crumbs and whining for his breakfast.

Heather nudged him with her ankle. "You'll eat in a minute." She leaned over to scratch his ears. The little pig rolled on his back, inviting her to scratch his belly, too.

Ben put a small helping of grain in a metal dish and set it in the mudroom. Pinky Pie was not a neat eater. Heather had to sweep the mudroom most days.

Ben watched the gobbling pig for a moment. Then he plopped himself in his chair for the first bite of warm oatmeal. Heather took out her cell phone and speed-dialed her best friend.

"Hi, Kathy! No school!"

She listened to the chortle of satisfaction on the other end of the line.

"What are you going to do? Go back to bed?"

"No way!" Kathy laughed. "I've got to dig a path so I can reach Tess. It's like a half mile over to the stable."

"Wish I could come and help. But I'm going to get Hendrik out and show him what snow is!"

"Fun! I bet he loves it! Oh, Mom's calling. I'll talk to you later."

Heather put her cell in her pocket, frowning. She knew that Kathy's mother was strict and didn't like Kathy to talk very long to her friends. Kathy never complained to Heather, but she often had to hang up quickly. When there was a chance for the two friends to go out together to ride, Kathy took it eagerly.

"Hup boy!" Heather pushed at the hindquarters of her big Friesian horse while she pulled at his halter with the other hand to turn him in his square stall. Hendrik swung his black head around towards her, as he obeyed the pull on his halter and walked behind Heather out of his stall. His big hooves made a solid clomping sound on the floorboards of the barn.

The other horses were already grained and watered and their stalls mucked out. Now Heather was going to show Hendrik what snow was. Born the previous spring, he had never seen it. He had been shipped in the fall to the farm, all the way from Holland, where Friesian horses are raised. At only seven months, he was already a very large horse, all black, with long black mane and tail. He had yet to be shod, so the soft snow was unlikely to ball inside the frogs of his hooves.

Hendrik saw the dazzle of white snow on the ground in the stable yard. His ears pricked forward, and he lowered his big head to sniff this strange stuff. Cold!

Heather led him forward. Hendrik walked easily through snow only a foot deep. He kept his head near Heather's shoulder, as she walked him down the driveway between trees that leaned over the plowed path with their white burdens. Only a few flakes were falling now.

She scooped a handful of snow and offered it to the young horse. Hendrik sniffed, then blew through his nostrils. The snowflakes scattered, some of them into Heather's face. She laughed and tossed more snow on his back. Hendrik was unruffled by a little snow on his warm coat. He nuzzled his wet nose into her neck scarf until she squealed.

"Come on, Hendrik!" As she led him further, Heather thought about Kathy. They often rode to school together in the Hobbes' old pickup truck. It would have been nice on a snow day to spend some time together. Kathy was starting to teach her horse, Tess, how to do dressage. Dressage takes a lot of training Heather mused. All those steps back and forth with tight control of the horse.

Thinking about it, she failed to watch for the birches that bowed down into the driveway, top-heavy with snow. The clomp of Hendrik's hooves vibrated through the ground, making a heavy load of snow land beside them, narrowly missing Heather's head. She got a shower of cold flakes on her hair, nonetheless, and shook them off, while the birches straightened slowly up again.

She couldn't ride Hendrik down the drive. He had never had a saddle on his back. He was still getting used to a bridle with a bit. But he was a very gentle horse and walked obediently whenever Heather led him by the halter.

They walked down the drive on the side that Heather's dad had plowed, before going on to plow driveways for other people before finishing his own. The dirt showed through the snow in places where Alan Hobbes' plow had scraped it. The drive wound downhill for half a mile through the snowy woods. Heather stopped and turned Hendrik before the end of the drive at the county road. She wouldn't expose him to fast traffic, especially when the road was slippery. Let him get used to snow first.

As they came back up the drive, the Hobbes' old farmhouse came into sight. It was built on posts, so every winter Heather helped her father bank the house against icy winds by laying plastic sheeting along the ground and nailing it to the posts. The woodstoves kept them warm and cozy inside when cold drafts didn't come up through the floors. Heather knew Kathy's house was much snugger. It was built into a hill, with windows only on the front, so there were no drafts along the floors.

The side door of the Hobbes' farmhouse opened, and Ben jumped out in the snow. He wore a down jacket, visor hat with earflaps, thick gloves, and heavy Maine packers on his feet with felt boot liners inside them. Between his legs scuttled Pinky Pie, who dashed excitedly through the snow toward Heather and Hendrik. Heather held Hendrik still while the pig frolicked around his legs. But Hendrik was used to Pinky Pie.

"He wanted to come with me!" shouted Ben. "How does Hendrik like snow?"

"Likes it fine!" Heather answered. She headed for the stable, leading Hendrik. Their breath made white clouds in the cold air. Pinky Pie's breath made a little cloud.

Their dad's plow had pushed a big snowdrift up beside the barn. "Whoopee!" shouted Ben. He threw himself into the soft snowdrift. Heather laughed as he emerged covered with white powder snow. "Better brush that off before you start lugging wood—I don't want it in the house!"

Ben flapped his jacket, spreading snow through the air. He shuffled a path over to the thermometer on the side of the barn. He brushed the snow off it and announced, "Only eighteen degrees! I'll warm up the pickup." Ben took any excuse to run the truck that Heather used for school and groceries.

Heather, with horse and pig following, was nearly to the stable door, when the motor of the truck parked by the stable came to life with a loud cough. Hendrik rose on his hind legs and pawed the air in alarm.

"Come on!" said Heather sharply. Holding on to Hendrik's halter with both hands, she was lifted off her feet in the air. Pinky Pie scooted away toward the house.

"You've heard the truck before!" she scolded, as her weight brought Hendrik's head back down, and her feet reached the ground.

Ben stepped out of the pickup, the motor still running. "Sorry!" he called, as he began to clear snow from the windows of the truck.

"It's OK," she called back, "he's learning about snow *and* trucks!"

Ben finished cleaning off the truck. Once he was sure the battery was strong in freezing weather, he turned the motor off and headed regretfully for the woodpile. He was not allowed to carry more than three logs at a time, so it took several trips to stack 24 hours worth of wood near the kitchen stove and the woodstove in the living room. Then he ran to fetch his skis.

Heather decided to put Hendrik in the paddock to tramp around in the snow. She wouldn't keep him inside until the temperature dropped another 20 degrees, which it would by January. Hendrik waited outside while Heather mucked out his stall and put fresh straw and a fresh bucket of water in it. When she led him back into it, after sweeping the walkway through the barn, he found fresh hay as well as water and got busy.

Heather wanted to call Kathy again, but she decided it would be wiser to wait until afternoon for a chat. Kathy's mother might go out, and her father would certainly be out with his plow. She went to look for Pinky Pie. She found him chewing on a bridle rein that hung too low from a hook in the tack room.

"Naughty!" she scolded him, hanging the reins higher. He cocked his head at her, jaws still busily working.

"What have you got?" She caught him under the chin and forced his jaws open. Fishing out a small piece of leather, she exclaimed, "One of these days, you're going to have a sick stomach. You're no goat!"

The little pig didn't look the slightest bit ashamed. He scolded right back at her with yips and squeals. Then he rolled over on his back so Heather could scratch his stomach.

Ben came in wearing boots for skiing and found his cross country skis where he remembered hanging them last March, on the wall in the tack room. He took a candle end out of his pocket and began coating the bottoms of the narrow skis with wax. Then he carried them outside and fitted his ski boots into the bindings.

Heather watched. "Aren't you going to take poles?"

"Nah. Don't need 'em." Ben was confident. He slid his feet back and forth a few times to test that his skis slid well. Then he was off around the paddock.

His skis sank into the deep snow, so Ben shuffled them with a running step across the field behind the barn. When he reached the woods, the layer of snow under the trees was thinner. Here he could glide along the trail. He thrust one foot out, keeping on his toes, then the other. This was the life!

The forest landscape looked different, deep in snow. Ben knew exactly where the trail led, having ridden horses along it all summer and fall. He kept to a steady pace, not too fast, to hold off the fatigue that sometimes hit him.

He saw tracks of a small creature: two small feet together in back and two larger hind feet apart in front—a rabbit. Why not look for its hole?

He turned from the trail and tried to wind his narrow skis between the white humps of rocks where the rabbit had hopped. With no poles, he soon lost his balance. Wind milling his arms desperately, he raised one leg. The point of his ski rammed through snow to the hard rock beneath. He heard the crack of wood. Then he was down, one arm flung out to break his fall.

Twenty minutes later he returned home, stomping heavily through the drifts, carrying his skis over his shoulder. The tip of one of them hung by a shred of wood. Heather was cleaning breakfast dishes in the kitchen and saw him through the window. She rushed outside.

"What happened?"

Ben looked disgusted. "Stupid ski! Got hung up on a rock."

"And you fell." Heather looked at the ripped sleeve of his snow jacket and the snow-covered figure that was her brother.

"Yeah." Ben seemed disinclined to discuss it further.

"How do you feel?" She watched him throw down his skis and take several deep breaths.

"I'm okay. I think. I'll just watch the tube a while."

Ben entered the mudroom and began to strip off wet outer clothing. Some of the white that fell off his jacket wasn't snow but down feathers. Heather knew better than to nag. Ben's heart told him when to rest. Good thing an appointment with the doctor was coming right up.

As she went to look up her sewing kit, the old feeling of depression came over her. How was she going to help her impetuous brother meet his challenges and get through life without serious damage? It seemed like too hard a task sometimes. Sometimes a horse had to be put down, if it had heart trouble. But it was her job to see that Ben's heart got everything it needed!

The next morning the sun was shining, the roads were plowed, and school was open. Ben took the school bus, but Heather, a senior, had a later schedule. When she pulled the pickup into Kathy's driveway, Heather saw her friend come out the side door of her house and walk toward her. Kathy was wearing a purple, goose down vest with a white furry collar and no hat.

"Hi!" she said, as she swung into the passenger seat. "How are things?"

"A fine snow day I had," grumped Heather. "Lots of chores and no riding. But I had fun with Hendrik. Did you work on dressage?"

"I did! For a while, that is." Kathy wrinkled her forehead. "Tess can move forward one step on signal, but, backwards is still a problem."

"When can you bring her over, so we can practice together?"

"Not soon. She still has her shoes, so I can't take her out in the snow. And a blacksmith visit to remove them costs a lot."

This was true. Heather let the matter drop, and they talked of school events until they reached the school parking lot.

A spell of warm weather arrived a few days later in early December. The snow cover on the fields shrank to less than four inches. The thaw caused the icicles on the edges of the barn roof to drip and shrink during the day, making puddles along the barn walls. At night the wet puddles froze again, and the wet snow on the fields formed a crust that turkeys could walk on.

One morning Heather looked out the window and saw them across the driveway. She opened the door, and Pinky Pie rushed out to join the turkeys. His little feet cut through the icy crust so his stomach rubbed on the snow. He grumbled and hopped around, but he loved to root in the snow with his snout while the turkeys were pecking at winter grass. Big Tom Turkey was a special friend. They walked together around the edge of the field, the turkey pecking, and the pig rooting.

The young turkeys in the flock were called jakes. Their feathers stuck out on their chests, making them look like pincushions. They followed Big Tom's lead, but they weren't sure about Pinkie Pie. Deer hunting season was over, but hunters were still out with muzzleloaders. Birds were always in season, but wild turkeys are a protected species in Maine. After a while, Heather called Pinky Pie to come indoors. She rattled his food dish.

Pinky Pie lifted his head, his ears pricked up. Then he scooted to the farmhouse and in through the door Heather held partly open. Before she could put his dish down in front of him, Pinky Pie spotted her Birkenstocks and took a nibble at a cute little toe poking out.

"Ow!" Heather dropped the dish. The pig's grain rattled on the mudroom floor. "You bit me!" She grabbed a piece of newspaper from the recycle stack, rolled it up, and took a whack at his hindquarters. Pinky Pie rushed around the mudroom, squealing, but avoiding the newspaper. Heather missed him several times. Then she gave up and tossed the paper on the floor. Pinky Pie at once sat on it and looked up at her, his head cocked. She began to laugh.

"Heather! Are we going now?" Ben stuck his head in the door of the mudroom. He was wearing a clean, long-sleeved shirt that matched his blue eyes, and his feet were in street shoes, instead of his packers or ski boots.

"Yes. I've got Pinky Pie inside, and Dad will do the horses when he gets back later." She kicked off her sandals and slipped into socks and heavy, laced shoe boots.

They climbed into the pickup and headed for the city, two hours drive to the south. Heather knew Ben was nervous. It was the day the doctor had promised to decide about his pacemaker. Their father had an important appointment and couldn't get back in time, so Heather and Ben were making the trip together.

Ben watched Heather steer the old truck easily down the icy drive and onto the fast road that led to the Interstate. He didn't want to think about his appointment with the doctor. Instead, he thought about how he would drive himself to appointments when he had his license. He dreamed of touring the roads, passing other cars, and honking at those who didn't move over to let him by. He would pick up his friends after school and just joyride around the state!

"Heather," he said, as an idea popped into his head.

"Yep." Heather's mind was on the snowy road.

"Heather, I'll be fifteen by the end of the month. Do you think Dad will let me get my license then? I'll be finished with driver's ed."

"I don't know," Heather said slowly. "It's a lot for you to handle—school work and sports and all. And driving in January is the worst."

"Would he let me if I make the honor roll? What if I pay for the insurance myself?"

Heather knew Ben had been saving his money.

"Insurance is awful expensive. I thought you were saving for a car?"

"This is more important. I bet I have enough. Would he, Heather, do you think he would?"

"Well, I guess," said Heather. "Dad probably will say OK. Though," she added, "he sure wasn't pleased you trashed your skis and your coat!"

Ben had no defense there. He looked at the patch Heather sewed on his jacket sleeve and sighed. But thoughts about his license helped the long ride to Portland pass quickly. Rather than thinking about falling with his skis or a possible operation on his chest, Ben concentrated on exactly how Heather used the levers and pedals in the truck. It was an old Chevy with a gearshift. Ben intended to know every part of the motor, so he could be a good mechanic when the time came for lubes and oil changes. When they drove into the city, Heather circled a block and found a parking space near the doctor's office.

They sat only a short time in the waiting room before the doctor saw them. He listened to Ben's chest with a stethoscope and told him to breathe deeply. He had Ben walk on a slow treadmill that tilted uphill. Finally, he told them he thought Ben was old enough now for a pacemaker.

"Only a minor operation," he told Ben, who was looking doubtful. "You won't miss much school." Now Ben looked disappointed. Heather chuckled.

They made an appointment for the pacemaker and got back in the pickup. It was almost dark outside, though it was only 3:30 in the afternoon. The headlights on the old pickup weren't the best, so Heather stayed in the right-hand lane on the Interstate.

She tried to concentrate on driving, but her thoughts drifted to Ben and his upcoming operation. Another trip to the city. Would Ben be OK until then? Should she keep him out of sports? He loved to ski, but all that pushing with the poles he now used couldn't be good. She hated to nag, but she felt responsible. She turned her head to speak to Ben and caught something out of the corner of her eye.

The brake lights were flashing in the car just ahead of them. It swerved madly to avoid a deer crossing the road. They could hear a loud thump as the car hit the deer.

Chapter Two

The car ahead skidded sideways and stopped with its front end off the highway and the back partly blocking the right hand lane. The deer was lying in the middle of the Interstate.

"Cripes!" Heather stamped on the brakes and pulled in carefully behind the stopped car on the side of the Interstate. She put on the flashers, then got out and ran to the driver's window. She knocked on it, but nobody responded. Passing cars were slowing down, veering around the deer and the stopped cars. Ben went to stand near the deer. He waved the oncoming traffic to the side of the highway.

Heather opened the driver's car door a little and said, "Are you OK? Are you hurt?" The girl in the driver's seat gasped and laughed and gasped and cried. She was having hysterics.

"Can you move your car?" Heather asked urgently.

There was no response but more gasps. Ben had followed Heather, and she turned to him.

"Ben! Take care of this girl and get her car off the road while I deal with the deer!"

Ben helped the girl move over and got in the driver's seat. He steered the car carefully so it was off the road. Then he turned off the motor and helped the weeping girl move back behind the wheel. He wished he had a driver's license!

Heather stood near the middle of the road, waving cars over to the left side of the road with a flashlight. The oncoming traffic swerved to avoid her and the deer. She pulled out her cell phone and dialed 911. She gave her name. "There's a deer down on the highway!"

"Where are you – northbound or southbound?"

"Northbound." Heather looked to the side of the highway. "At mile 121."

"We'll have someone there as soon as possible."

One of the passing cars slowed and stopped. Heather saw with relief that two men were getting out of their pickup.

"Can you help get this deer off the road?" she asked them. One man stood with his hands in his pockets, gazing at the deer, while the other one took over the job of gesturing at cars that slowed down when they saw the group on the road.

The first man shook his head. "That deer's still alive," he announced. "Still got one antler. He's dangerous. I'm not getting hooked."

Heather looked at him with exasperation. "Come on! If we all take hold of him, we can move him at least! He's going to get hit again here on the road!"

The man continued to shake his head. After a little while, he and the other man got back in their car and drove on. Heather looked after them, her temper rising. *At least Ben has that girl calmed down and off the road. I guess this one is up to me. Poor girl! Poor deer!*

During a pause in the traffic, she approached the deer. Its eyes were closed, but now and then, it twitched all over, and its legs shook. It was a fine animal. What a shame the deer in Maine had to share the road with cars.

Heather knew there are few places on a deer's body it can't reach with its rack. Drawing a deep breath, she put one hand on the deer's remaining antler and the other under its head. Then, watching for cars, she dragged the heavy animal over the icy road into the mid-strip between the lanes of the highway.

What do I do now? Put it out of its misery? Break its neck? It was going to be a hard decision for Heather.

A large flatbed truck pulled over to the roadside behind Heather's pickup. The driver got out and set a flare to warn other cars. Then he came over to where she stood by the deer.

"Guess this one's a goner," he remarked. He had a gun in his hand. "Shall I finish him?"

"Yes, please! I was afraid I'd have to break his neck." Heather looked regretfully at the beautiful deer.

The man leveled his gun at the deer's head and pulled the trigger once. As the shot resounded, the deer went limp. They both looked at it. "Too bad," said the unknown man, "You wouldn't believe how often this happens. You can be glad it wasn't a moose." He stood silent a few minutes, then, "Well, I got to be going."

Heather lifted a hand in farewell, as he got back in his big truck. She would have to wait for the trooper, having given her name. She checked that Ben and the girl were OK and then stood in the cold by the deer, feeling glad she had on her warm shoes. Finally, a state trooper pulled up with flashing lights on his car.

"You hit a deer?" he asked, as soon as he saw Heather by the deer. He began to write on a pad.

"No. That person in the red car hit him," said Heather. "I just pulled him off the road."

"Looks like he's dead," said the trooper, prodding the deer's body with his flashlight.

"Yes, he was alive when I moved him, but a driver came along and shot him."

"What!" yelled the trooper, "Who did it? Where is he?"

"He went on his way," replied Heather. "After all, it took you 45 minutes to get here."

"Never mind that!" snapped the officer, "Nobody lets a gun off and leaves the scene. Describe him for me."

Heather's temper exploded. Speaking quietly but intensely, she made it clear that she had done nothing but report the accident and wait in the cold, that her young brother was trying to comfort a hysterical driver who needed help, and that the man with the gun had rendered service by making it unnecessary for her to strangle a deer! Would he like her to write it out and send it in to the paper and the chief of police, who is a personal friend? Would he mind if she took her brother home now, as he was due for a pacemaker next month? Should they perhaps see if the driver who hit the deer needed medical help?

She drew another breath to go on, but the trooper held up both hands. "OK, OK, I got you," he said, "Just give me a few details, and I'll take it from there." He followed her over to the red car. Politeness dripped from his lips, as he consulted with the young driver, who was huddled under Ben's arm. Soon they were all free to go.

"You know what, Heather?" Ben exclaimed, as they drove away, "She's only a high school freshman! She just got her driver's license! What bad luck to hit a deer her first time out alone!"

"Good lesson for somebody," muttered Heather. She was still simmering over her brush with the arrogant trooper. But, as her temper cooled and her toes warmed, she thought again about Ben getting a license and the dangers of the road.

Ben felt lucky. He didn't make a single mistake on the written driver's test. Of course, he had memorized the whole driver's manual, so the questions were a snap. The road test wasn't hard either. Heather had warned him about the boy who let the wheels of the car roll at a stop sign. Ben made sure the pickup came to a full halt at every stop sign.

The trooper who tested Ben congratulated him.

"Not many kids do this well. I think you'll be a careful driver. And you're lucky that your birthday came before they put the driving age up to sixteen."

Ben wore a broad grin when he rejoined Heather at the motor vehicle office.

"I'm driving home!" he announced, waving his interim license. Heather gave him a hug.

"You're the chauffeur," she laughed and even let him drive without making a single suggestion.

In January, the temperature dropped to minus ten. The barn had a large, indoor arena with a dirt floor. While it was so cold, Heather put all the horses in the arena to mill around, until they were led to their stalls in the evening. Hay rigs (small racks) were strung up at intervals along the side of the eighty-foot arena. Each horse had its own rig.

Draft horses are bred with Thoroughbreds to get "sport" horses. These horses lift their knees high like draft horses and can be well trained in dressage, a very disciplined style of riding. Ally was a sport horse. He was a chestnut and as large as Hendrik, the Friesian. The two males liked to be together, even though Ally was seven years older than Hendrik.

A white mare named Sugar wanted to be with Hendrik and was jealous of Ally. She left her hay rig and began eating from Hendrik's, side by side with him. If Ally came near, she needled him by nipping at his side. She didn't seem to realize that Ally, with his weight and cocked horseshoes, could lame her for life.

Sugar was still recovering from a sore on one of her hocks that happened when a fence got in her way. She was a dainty little horse that could wheel and circle quickly. Now she had to wear bell boots, like cardboard cones on her feet to keep them from rubbing against the sore. At night in Sugar's stall, Heather spread salve on Sugar's hock and fed her medicine. Sugar didn't like the powdered medicine. Heather thought of mixing it with applesauce—Sugar liked that!

Heather sucked up the applesauce with the medicine in a big bulb baster before putting it in Sugar's mouth. Just then, Ally put his great head over the partition between his stall and Sugar's. He was curious. Heather showed him the bulb baster. Ally smelled the applesauce. He grabbed the baster with his teeth. Heather laughed and squirted the applesauce into Ally's mouth. When he had swallowed it, he licked the baster in appreciation.

Sugar was indignant. "That's my medicine," she seemed to say. She nudged Heather and opened her mouth. Heather wondered how long it would take for Sugar's hock to heal. She enjoyed riding the quick little horse. As she sucked up the last of the applesauce with the baster, an idea began to form in her head.

"Tess is a beauty!"

Heather was helping Kathy groom her grey mare in the small stall in the little stable that Kathy's father had built. It was located down the road about a hundred yards from the family house. Kathy's mother couldn't stand the smell of manure.

"I love Tess." Kathy buried her face in the soft mane a moment, then continued to pull a currycomb through the thick hair the horse had grown in the cold months.

"She's so quick." Heather remembered her idea. "Kathy, do you think you could teach her to do team-penning? I've got Sugar trained now so she can whip around the big oil cans when I put them out in the arena."

Kathy considered the question. "I could certainly start showing her the ropes. But are you thinking of competing?"

"We'd need a third rider if we did. But I don't think there's ever been women in the team-penning competition. We'd be the first!"

Kathy looked excited. "Wow! But I'd have to work Tess up to it. And then convince my folks to let me."

"Ok. Start with wheeling her when you take her out. The next time you're over to us, we'll try it with two horses around the can."

"That's cool!" Kathy gave Tess a final pat and closed the stall half-door behind her. She leaned on it, gazing at her beloved Tess. "Can we start tomorrow? The trails over to your place are still too snowy, but I could bring her in the old trailer."

"Well, I promised Ben's teacher to do something with his class. Perhaps the day after."

Ben's class was taking an afternoon bus trip to Cadillac Mountain on Mount Desert Island. After school, Heather waited at the bus stop outside the school to join Ben's class. Mrs. Bellam had asked Heather to accompany the class on a sleigh ride. She knew Heather was a good person to have around horses.

Heather watched Ben's class mill around at the top of a snowy slope by the school parking lot. One of the boys had a jumpbumper. A jumpbumper is a backless seat on a single ski or runner. It takes good balance to ride on it. The boy ran toward the top of the slope, whipped the jumpbumper under himself and slid down the hill with his feet in the air while his friends gave encouraging whoops. He made it halfway down before he fell off in the snow. Heather saw it was Ben. He dusted himself off and handed the jumpbumper to another boy, who made it all way down the hill to cheers.

Mrs. Bellam came hurrying out of the school, wrapped in scarves. "Hello, Heather!" she said in relief, when she saw her. Heather answered, "Hi, Mrs. Bellam" and followed the class onto the bus. Ben and the rest of the boys crowded into the rear of the bus. Heather sat beside a girl who was seated alone.

The bus driver took them along snowy side roads until they reached the interstate, which was well plowed. Heather was chatting with her seatmate. She became aware of whispers and laughter behind her. Then she heard a rough, grating sound. Mrs. Bellam was chatting with the bus driver. Heather got up quickly and strode to the rear.

"OK, you guys!" She held out her hand. "Let's have them right now!"

"Aw, Heather!" There was a general wail. With one hand on her hip, Heather stared down the two boys who sat in front of the rear window. She knew them—Shank and Woody—nice boys, but risk-takers. She waited with her hand out, tapping the toe of her boot. Finally, Woody shrugged and handed over a small cigarette lighter. Heather put it in her pocket and held out her hand again, this time to Shank.

"Awww." Shank came up with a tiny lighter shaped like a gun. Heather pocketed it without comment. She collected a few more lighters from other boys, including Ben. He looked a little cross. "What are you gonna do, Heather?"

"I'll return them when we're back at school."

Heather went back to her seat, her pockets bulging. She'd have to unload the lighters somewhere safe before the sleigh ride. Ben's friends looked at him. They knew Heather was almost like Ben's mother.

"You got a tough sister," Shank said to Ben.

"Yeah," said Ben, "my dad's tough, too."

"My dad's tough, too—when I see him," said Woody.

Ben bragged, "One time, when Heather had a party, Dad just went around with a big bowl and made everyone toss in their car keys. Wouldn't let anyone have them back when they left until he smelled their breath!"

The boys told movie plots until they reached Mount Desert. The bus drew up in a large parking lot, near a ski shop. Ben would have liked to go in and look at cross-country skis, but the class was climbing into two sleighs, each drawn by a large farm horse. He guessed they were Clydesdales. Running, he squeezed into the last space in the first sleigh where Shank and Woody were already munching on popcorn that Mrs. Bellam passed out. Heather left the cigarette lighters with the driver and climbed into the back of the second sleigh which most of the girls had chosen.

Each sleigh had a driver who climbed up to high seats above where the students were crowded together on the straw-covered floors. Bells jingled as they started off. The boys gave whoops of excitement.

The first horse turned onto a wide carriage drive that wound around the base of Cadillac Mountain. The air was crisp and cold. Woody and Shank ate all their popcorn before they remembered to save some for a popcorn fight. Then they teased Ben for some of his.

"Aw, come on—you can't eat all of that!" coaxed Woody. Shank simply reached over for Ben's bag.

"Hey! Cut that out!" Ben nimbly evaded Shanks's grab. He hunched over the side of the sleigh, eating his popcorn in a hurry. He noticed there were double tracks along the carriage drive for cross country skiers, but the sleighs stayed off to the side of the drive, so the sleigh runners and horses' hooves wouldn't spoil the skiing tracks. Ben planned to come back sometime and ski the carriage drive.

The woods were quiet and filled with snow. The sleighs were full of noisy chatter. Mrs. Bellam had a bunch of girls singing "Jingle Bells." Ben pointed out rabbit tracks in the snow. Everyone was enjoying the ride.

They were deep in the woods, crossing a wooden bridge, when the sleigh in front stopped. The horse was making loud neighing sounds. Ben leaned out to see what the matter was. Heather jumped down from her sleigh and ran forward. She found the big Clydesdale in front had put his foot through a rotten plank in the bridge. He was struggling to pull it out.

"Come here," Heather called to the second driver. "Ben, go and hold his horse!"

Ben was out on the snowy drive in a flash. He knew how to approach the uneasy horse slowly before taking hold of its bridle.

The two drivers talked with Heather. She told one of them to unhitch the crippled horse from the sleigh and the other one to hold on to his bridle near his mouth. The big brown horse was shivering with fear and pain. Heather could see his leg was bleeding where he repeatedly jerked it against the boards of the bridge.

She began to stroke his leg and talk to him. "Keep his head down," she whispered to the young man who was holding him. "Have you got a jackknife on you?"

She took the knife the young man held out and opened it. The horse had thick horsefeathers, as the long hair around the hooves is called. The horsefeathers on the hoof below the boards of the bridge seemed to be caught on something. Carefully she cut them away, until the big hoof came free. Then she helped ease it up out of the hole.

"Easy, boy," she whispered to the nervous horse, as he backed away from the hole and tried his weight on his hoof. She crouched by his front leg and ran her hand down it.

"Lead him forward," she said. "Let's see if he limps." The driver clicked his tongue and pulled on the bridle. "C'mon Standard," he coaxed. Standard was afraid to pass the hole with the rotten wood. "Can you back him off the bridge?" asked Heather.

"Not until we move both sleighs," said the driver.

Heather gave the jackknife back and trudged over to speak to Mrs. Bellam. Soon all of Ben's class was helping push first one, then the other sleigh backwards away from the bridge, while Ben backed the horse whose bridle he was holding. Mrs. Bellam smiled at him.

"It's great that you and your sister know how to handle horses!" she exclaimed.

"We still have to get back," Ben answered. "That bridge doesn't seem safe."

Heather was walking across the bridge, jumping on it here and there. Her heavy boots bounced on the planks.

"What have you been feeding your horse?" she said to the driver, a tall, redheaded young man with freckles. "This bridge will never hold him."

He smiled at her. "My name's Russ. I don't feed Standard, I just drive him sometimes in the winter."

"Looks like we got to get two horses and sleighs turned around on this trail."

"Yep," he agreed. "There's a clearing a little way back. "Be easier to push the loose sleigh there before we hitch up Standard again. But it's an uphill push."

The other driver took over the horse whose bridle Ben was holding. He began the tricky task of turning the horse and sleigh around in a small clearing. Ben joined the rest of the class and helped turn the sleigh around. But even 25 young pairs of arms and legs couldn't turn the loose sleigh around. For that, they needed Standard.

Russ walked Standard slowly up the hill, speaking soothingly to him. The big horse walked evenly without limping, even though there was blood on his leg. Russ backed Standard into the shafts of the sleigh, and in no time Standard had the sleigh turned around. "Good boy!" Heather and Russ said at the same time. They laughed in relief. Soon the sleighing party was on the way home to pizza and hamburgers. Woody looked at Ben with new respect. "You sure know horses!" Shank just shrugged.

Russ called to Heather, "Like to ride up beside me?" They chatted all the way back.

CHAPTER THREE

KATHY BEGAN BRINGING TESS regularly to the Hobbes' arena for team-penning practice. Her Tess was intelligent and learned quickly from Heather's horse, Sugar. Sugar was small-footed and quick, which is why Heather chose her to do team penning. To cut cows out of a herd and move them across a line in an arena, a horse has to dart and swerve and stop quickly. The rider has to be able to stay on the horse while it changes direction rapidly. Heather was quite pleased with Sugar and Tess by the end of that day's training. They had practiced with oilcans, placed at intervals in the arena. Heather would race Sugar to an oilcan, circle it in one way, circle it in the other, stop suddenly, and race back to the starting line that she drew on the arena floor. Then Kathy and Tess would repeat the maneuver.

When they stopped for a rest, Kathy asked, "Have you thought of anyone to ride with us?"

"Well, I had an idea. What do you think about Chrissy?"

Kathy looked dubious. "I know she's got a horse. And lots of money. Question is: has she got guts?"

"She might lack confidence some. But you get that with practice. Shall I ask her?"

Kathy paused, then nodded. "Call her now." She watched while Heather made a pitch to Chrissy on her cell phone. When the phone was back in Heather's pocket, she said, "And?"

"She's hesitant, more interested in dressage than what we're doing. But she said she'd bring Silver over and see what it involves."

"Well, Sheesh."

"I know. But I can't think of anyone else. It would be some deal if we entered the competition. Just use the first letters of our first names, so no one knows we're not men."

Kathy hooted and gave a thumbs-up.

One Friday night the phone rang. Ben answered it and came to ask if he could drive some friends to a MacDonald's.

"They just want a lift," he explained. "It's Woody and Shank—you met them on the bus. We won't be out long."

Heather was writing a term paper, her head bent over the family computer. "OK," she mumbled absently, then looked up. "Better be home before ten. We have to get up for early chores. And be sure your cell is charged."

"It is! I will!" Ben was out the door in a flash.

It was two hours later when the phone rang again. Heather left the computer wearily and picked it up.

"Is this Heather?" inquired a man's voice. "I guess your dad is away, isn't he? This is Chief of Police Arnold. Could you come down to the station? We've got a little problem here."

Ben! Heather's heart was in her throat. For once her dad had gone by taxi and left his car at home. She grabbed his keys from a hook by the door, as she ran out of the house. Pinky Pie yipped in protest from the mudroom where she had closed him.

At the police station, Woody, Shank, and Ben were slumped on a bench together. They didn't open their mouths to say anything when Heather walked by. "You Ok?" she asked Ben. He just nodded. She went with the police chief to his office.

"Sorry, Heather, but this is pretty serious," the chief said when the door was closed. He placed a chair for her by his desk.

"What sort of serious?" Heather had seen that Ben looked sad but not damaged in any way.

"Look at these." He spread some five-dollar bills out on his desk.

Heather looked at them, then at the chief. "Stolen?" she asked, a lump in her throat.

"No, it's worse. They're counterfeit."

Heather goggled at him. "Counterfeit? They look real!"

"They're cleverly done – the right paper in a copy machine – but, yes, they're not made by Uncle Sam."

"What—how did they turn up?" Heather was white now. Counterfeiting was a federal crime!

"Someone with sharp eyes at the MacDonald's. The worker was positive they came from the table where the boys sat. We're calling the parents before we question them, Heather. I know you're standing in for your dad, so I called you first."

Heather thought a minute. She faced the chief. "I want to state right now: there's absolutely no way those bills could have come from our place. There's just no way Ben could have produced them."

"I know." The chief wore a kindly expression. "We'll get it figured out."

"Ben told me the other two asked him for a ride to the place. He's a licensed driver, and they're not."

That was the story Ben told, when the chief questioned him in Heather's presence. He had no clue, he said, that the money for hamburgers wasn't real.

They waited while the other boys and their parents were in the chief's office. Woody's mother was crying when she came out. She was by herself, as her husband had abandoned her and Woody a few years back.

Shank's father was an angry-looking man. Ben told Heather in a whisper that Shank and his father had only just moved to Maine from some other state. He felt sorry for Shank, who had paid for their hamburgers.

When the interviews were finished, Ben drove home alone, behind Heather. The other boys left with their parents. Heather knew what Ben was thinking. *Here he just got his license, and he winds up in the police station! He must feel stupid! And nervous about getting his pacemaker put in next week! But he didn't know about the money. Did Shank know? Where did he get it, I wonder? And his father looked so mad! I'm sure Dad will understand when we tell him how it was.*

February was arena time for the horses. The snow was four feet deep outside and the temperature usually below zero. Chrissy had decided she would teach Silver team-penning, so the three girls practiced on weekends and occasional afternoons after school in the Hobbes' big indoor arena. Chrissy drove up to the stable, her shiny, new trailer attached to her SUV. She wore jodhpurs and looked elegant with long blond hair and black velvet jacket when she mounted her white horse, but both she and Silver were nervous about close work with other horses. Chrissy and Silver would ride to the end of the arena, wheel quickly around one oil can, while Heather and Sugar circled one at a distance. Then they would return to where they started. Heather gradually brought the oil cans closer together, so that Silver and Sugar nearly brushed each other when they circled. Then she began adding Tess to the mix.

Silver was willing to circle the cans alone, but sometimes she nipped at the other horses if they came near and shied. Once she balked and Chrissy came off and landed on the dirt floor. She was furious, her beautiful jodhpurs caked with mud and straw.

"That blasted horse!"

"You were doing great, Chrissy," Heather tried to soothe her. But Chrissy said that was all for the day and took Silver to her trailer.

"Is this going to work?" Kathy was doubtful.

"She's come a long way. I think we'll be good enough to compete by the time of the fair." Heather tried to sound confident.

In March, there were blizzards, but they melted quickly, leaving brown mud everywhere. Ben carried a lot of wood—and mud—indoors every day. He was sleepy in the morning. It was hard to get him out of bed. Sometimes he left his chores for Heather to do, slamming out the door and down to the main road to catch the school bus. He would have preferred to ride to school in the truck with Heather, but, as a senior, she was taking classes at the Community College on certain days and had a different schedule. Out in the cold air, he felt good running. The pacemaker in his chest was helping him breathe better. It was just that he felt so sleepy when he woke up.

Heather told herself he was growing, when she had to call him three times to get out of bed. But it was a pain not to have his help before she got herself to classes. And when they lost electricity, because ice on the trees toppled them on the wires, the pump didn't work, and they had to keep their drinking and washing water in a barrel lined with plastic on the porch. Overnight, ice formed on the top of the barrel. When she made breakfast, she had to break the ice and hold a gallon jug down in the freezing water to fill it. Cold fingers! It was really Ben's job, but he was running out of the house again, with his coat undone, his books under his arm, and a hunk of cheese between his teeth!

She had to admit that the pacemaker operation had been a success. With not many days lost, Ben had been back in school afterward, gradually increasing his activities, as he felt able to do so. He was only restricted in the weight he could lift, so Heather was carrying the wood until he got stronger.

On the way to school, Ben usually sat with Woody and Shank in the rear of the bus. Shank was living at Woody's house. His father had disappeared, and his mother had been gone for years. Ben sometimes brought treats to share with the other two boys. That morning, when he was fishing in his backpack for stray candy, he pulled out something that was not candy.

"Hey, look!" he said to his friends, "Look what was hanging around in my backpack!" He held out his hand with an unspent shell on it—a bullet for a hunting rifle.

"I must have left it there after I hunted with my dad last fall," he laughed. The other boys examined the shell, making small explosive noises. Shank pretended to aim it at a girl who was watching, and she ducked, squealing. Then Ben dropped it back in his backpack.

He didn't think any more about it, until he was called to the principal's office. He was surprised to see Mr. Commons looking at him seriously.

"Ben, I have a report that you have brought ammunition to school. Is this true?"

"Gee, Mr. Commons," said Ben, "I just found this leftover shell in my backpack. Should I throw it away or something?"

"No! Give it to me!"

Ben had to go to his locker and retrieve the shell. Returning to the office, he handed it to Mr. Commons. To his astonishment, he heard from the principal that he was to go home and stay there for three days!

"Can I take homework with me?" he asked, unhappy that he was once again in trouble.

"Yes, you can fetch your books. Then wait here in the office until Heather can drive you home. Really, Ben," the principal added, "Three days suspension is not a lot for bringing something like this into a school setting. You should know better."

Ben could hardly look Heather in the face when she arrived in the office after school. She had a glint in her eye. First the skis, then the police station, and now a three-day suspension! Ben tried to look confident and positive about not knowing school rules about ammunition.

"Guess you'll be doing a lot of homework," is all Heather said. But he could guess that she was smoldering inside.

On the weekend, Ben sat at the kitchen table and did three days worth of math, English composition, and history. Heather was out in the barn, working Sugar. She concentrated on the horse's moves, trying not to worry about Ben. She was still upset over his mishaps. Falling with his skis now seemed a trivial matter. He had come close to involvement in the federal crime of counterfeiting, and then, to get suspended for bringing a shell to school! Shoot! She wasn't his mother! She couldn't protect him from every stupid tangle a young boy found himself in! Heather blinked back tears and bit her lip. It would all go by, she knew. And she couldn't be a real mother to Ben. But she couldn't help feeling partly responsible when he got into trouble. She took a deep breath and clicked her tongue at Sugar, who was dancing in a circle.

Heather felt better after the hard workout. As she strode across the stable yard, she put her chin up to feel the wind around her neck. She had clipped off her long, chestnut hair the week before and given it to the wig makers for cancer patients, just as her mother had done, years before, before getting cancer herself. She just wanted to look different now. Her head felt light without the heavy hank of hair. When she had her white, wide-brimmed cowboy hat on, her short hair curled around her face. She would wear cowboy boots and jeans with her old brown chaps, and a leather vest, too, when she took Sugar to the team penning contest. She needed to enlist her dad's support for that.

She saw him pulling his car into the old shed he used as a garage. Heather waved and waited for him to swing the shed door shut. They walked over the icy driveway into the farmhouse together. She told her dad about the upcoming event.

"You know Kathy and Chrissy have been practicing team-penning with me. Kathy works with Tess, a quarter horse, and Chrissy rides her mare, Silver. We compete against each other at practice, but we'd like a chance to compete together at the Fair."

"This would be the Farmington County Fair?" her dad asked.

"Yes. I talked the other girls into going as a team."

"Isn't that event for the men's teams?"

"It always has been. They're like professionals at it. They've never had women in there competing before."

"Guess I'll have to see this." Her dad gave her shoulder a squeeze, as they entered the kitchen. Ben was there, his head bowed low over his English paper. He didn't have much to say since his suspension from school.

Heather got a pan down to heat up some hash and asked, "Can Ben come to the Fair too?" She was both angry with her brother and a little sorry for him. Their dad had been displeased about the stray shell in Ben's backpack. He had added a curfew to Ben's restrictions and was a little stiff when he spoke to him. She was relieved when he nodded.

"We'll sit together, so I can keep an eye on him. Next thing, he'll be out there, team-penning with you!"

Ben just shook his head, but Heather laughed. "This is going to be a girl thing. Wait and see, we've practiced hard!"

In the next few weeks, Heather and Kathy, became better acquainted with Chrissy. She attended a private school, so they only saw her for team-penning practice on weekends and now and then after school. As they neared the day of the contest, Silver became used to wheeling and circling and stopping near Sugar and Tess. She didn't shy or nip at them, and Chrissy gave her frequent praise under Heather's instruction.

Chrissy began dropping over to Kathy's house to do homework together or just chat about their horses. As the friendship built between them, Chrissy seemed steadier as she guided Silver, and she laughed more often. Heather was pleased at the way the team was pulling together, even if she sometimes grudged Chrissy the time and attention she got from Kathy.

When the day came, the Hobbes family drove to the fair in their dad's car, a big SUV that had a ball hitch for the horse trailer. Sugar was used to the trailer, so Heather rode in the SUV with her dad and Ben. When they parked at the fairgrounds, she got out and backed Sugar down the ramp and out of the trailer. Sugar whickered when she saw other horses being fitted out in the parking lot. Ben held Sugar while Heather put on her chaps over her jeans. The chaps were brown leather with long fringes and only covered the front of her legs. With her studded leather vest and big hat, Heather looked great, Ben thought. Their dad got out his camera.

"Now just hold on a minute! I've got to record this momentous event!"

Heather put her saddle on Sugar and posed, standing by Sugar's head with the reins in her hand under Sugar's chin. After the camera flashed, she hugged her dad and Ben. They gave her V signs for Victory. Then she led Sugar away to find Kathy and Chrissy. They were busy gearing up their horses in the pen outside the stadium where the team penning took place.

"Everything OK?" she asked them.

Kathy lifted a gloved hand in greeting. "I think so. Chrissy's trying to calm Silver down. They're both nervous. So am I! What a team!"

She patted her own horse, Tess, on the neck and checked that her saddle girth was tight one more time.

Heather kept Sugar back from where Silver was dancing at the end of her reins.

"Better get her head down, talk to her," she advised.

Chrissy bit her lip, as she shortened the reins and took Silver next to the bit. She spoke in a hasty undertone to the high-strung mare. Soon Silver was able to stand still, her head down by Chrissy's shoulder. The three girls led their mounts to a side rail of the holding pen. Heather tied Sugar and went to find out the order they would compete in.

"We're first," she announced, when she returned.

"Drat!" Chrissy exclaimed, "Why couldn't we come last? At least I could see what the others do!"

Kathy smiled at her. "You'll be OK. Let's just get this done."

Just then, a team of three men entered the pen with their horses. "Well, looky here! Who do you think's going to ride 'em fast in this event? Need an hour or two, girls?"

The speaker smirked at them, while his buddies roared with laughter.

"Don't get your hopes up," Heather said coldly.

Alan Hobbes paid admission for himself and Ben at the stadium gate, and they found seats in the high stands. A big crowd of people, who came to the fair for the equestrian events, milled around the aisles and seats of the big, indoor arena.

Ben looked around. He saw the wide, tall door where the riders would enter the arena. He guessed the space was about the size of a football field. There was a line drawn across the dirt-filled floor at one end of the arena.

"What's that line for?" he asked his dad, pointing.

"That's where each team waits while they shout the numbers of the cows they have to corral. Then it's whoever gets their cows back across the line in the shortest time."

His dad's voice didn't sound cross like when they had it out about Ben's loose shell. Ben thought it sounded more like his usual friendly self. Crowded together on the stadium bench, their shoulders touched. Perhaps all would be well.

They watched while a group of fifteen cows were brought into the arena and allowed to move freely about. Each cow had a number tied on both its sides. Then Heather, Kathy, and Chrissy rode their horses in and brought them to the area beyond the line. A voice over a loudspeaker announced "The Lazy D Riders!" The timer was alerted with a gong, and three numbers were shouted.

Heather tried to shout at Chrissy which number she should go for, but Silver had shot forward on the gong, and Chrissy was trying to hold the nervous horse. Heather caught up to her and yelled, "You take number ten!" Then she neck-reined Sugar over to cut out cow number three and herd it back across the line. Kathy and Tess were already almost there with a cow, but Chrissy was still trying to find her cow. Heather left cow number three behind the line and went to help. Together they succeeded in driving cow number ten across the line.

At that moment Heather realized that her own cow number three had strayed back across the line toward the herd. When she finally succeeded in catching up to it and returning with it to the others, they knew their time was high.

"Four minutes," the announcer called, sounding bored.

The Lazy D team left the arena, their faces downcast.

"OK," Heather stated, when they were outside the building and had dismounted. "That wasn't so hot, I know. But we can do much better, now we've done it once. We'll have another chance."

Kathy said, "We're not acting like a team yet. We need to work on that." Chrissy said nothing. She tossed her long, blond hair over her shoulder, as she walked Silver away from them towards her trailer.

"If we've still got a team," said Heather.

Kathy looked after Chrissy. "Her parents let her do anything. You wouldn't believe the hoops I had to jump, just to be here, let alone compete." Heather reached out a hand in comfort, and Kathy gave it a squeeze.

"I didn't see her folks. Did you?"

"No. They're probably above such low-class doings." Kathy tried to smile, but her mouth turned down at the corners.

"Let's go find her." Heather tugged at Kathy's hand.

Kathy nodded. They went to find Chrissy's SUV and trailer. Chrissy had put Silver in the trailer and was sitting on the bumper, crying.

"Hey teammate." Heather touched Chrissy's arm tentatively. Kathy's heart seemed to melt. She sat next to Chrissy and put her arm around her shoulders.

"Hey, it's OK. You did your best. We all flubbed—slow as molasses. Not your fault."

Chrissy raised streaming eyes. "You don't know. I wish I could, but I just can't."

She seemed so alone. Heather looked around. She didn't think Chrissy's folks had come to the fair. Maybe they were looking for her.

"Are your mom and dad here somewhere?" she asked gently, with a stroke on Chrissy's arm.

"Are you kidding? They'd never come to a county fair. I didn't even tell them about it." The tears rolled down her face. "They just give me money to do what I want. They don't care."

Heather thought of her dad and Ben, probably waiting for her right now, as the cheering in the arena seemed to have died down. Kathy was whispering in Chrissy's ear. She gave her a little hug and stood up.

"Come on," she announced. "It's time for this team to have a little celebration. We entered the competition, didn't we? We competed didn't we? We got those darn cows where they had to be. Now we deserve some good food."

She marched Chrissy across the fairgrounds to a food tent, while Heather followed, marveling at Kathy's ability to take charge. Compassion was Kathy's strong suit, whether for horses or humans. After ordering, Heather ran back to the arena to tell her dad and brother where she was. They joined the other girls, and everyone stuffed themselves with pizza. With renewed confidence, Heather, Kathy, and Chrissy began to discuss how they could team-pen better.

CHAPTER FOUR

HENDRIK WAS TEN MONTHS old in March. He already weighed 1400 pounds. When he clomped into the barn behind Heather, the floor resounded and his thick horsefeathers jingled with icy dingleberries. She decided he was old enough to learn about saddles and riders.

That afternoon, she began lessons for Hendrik by putting a blanket across his back. Hendrik looked around at it and pawed at his belly with his hind hoof, but the blanket didn't come off. He gave his attention to his hay rig.

Next, Heather added weight to the blanket. She tied Hendrik to his hay rig, so he would stand still. Then she stood on an upended crate and leaned on the horse's back, as though she were grooming him. Hendrik went on munching hay. Heather gave a hop and lay face down over his back. Hendrik moved uneasily, but he knew his owner. He followed Heather like a dog when he was loose, so he put up with her lying on his back.

Heather got off his back and patted him. She brought him a saddle to inspect. Hendrik sniffed at the leather saddle. He seemed ready for anything.

Heather reached high and swung the saddle over his back - and Hendrik spooked! He sidled and turned and tried to rear, spinning on his hind legs. The saddle landed on the floor of his stall. The end of the hay rig came off the wall.

"Okay, boy," Heather soothed him. She showed him the saddle again and rubbed it on his side. Hendrik's ears went back, but he stood still. Heather tried again to put the saddle on his back. She wanted Hendrik to understand that she intended to load him with this thing that fitted over his spine and dangled down both his sides. Hendrik pulled on his rope and moved his body next to the wall.

The hay rig was in danger of coming right off the wall. Heather gave it up for the day. But the lessons continued. Within a week, Hendrik was saddled.

Ben's friend, Woody, came over to see the horses and Pinky Pie. Shank wasn't with him, because Social Services were trying to reunite Shank with his mother and had set up an appointment in another state. Ben fetched Woody with the pickup. The driving age had changed to sixteen in the last month. Even though Woody was fifteen, like Ben, he couldn't get his license yet. He was envious, as Ben casually drove him back to the horse farm.

They found Pinky Pie in the house, where Heather and Kathy were treating him with bits of bread. When Pinky Pie got a treat, the cat, Tails, came to get one too. The pig and the cat were pals. They were about the same size. Heather put some oil from a can of tuna fish on a piece of bread for the cat. The cat picked at it daintily. When Kathy gave Pinky Pie a piece of bread, he gobbled it down.

Woody and Ben watched them. "What a pair! Does the pig do what you tell him to, here indoors?"

"Mostly," said Heather. "Except when it's bedtime. Then I have to use the broom to put him in the mudroom. He doesn't like to go to bed."

"So you sweep him off to bed!" exclaimed Kathy.

Heather laughed. "You could say that."

Ben took his friend off to view the horses. As the weather turned warmer—mostly above freezing—the horses spent more time in the paddock. There were five of them now. A roan gelding, named Chester, was being boarded for a girl who hoped to build her own barn and paddock.

The other new horse was the feisty little mare, named Silver, who belonged to Chrissy, Heather's team penning mate. Ben told Woody that Chrissy had moved her from another stable where equine disease had broken out. The horses at that stable were dying after a thoughtless owner had brought two contaminated horses there.

"Equine disease is terrible," Ben said. "The horses get exposed to it, and then they get too weak to stand up, and they fall down and die."

"Wow!" Woody was amazed. "Are you sure this horse that came from there is OK?"

"You bet. It's been tested."

They watched the horses roaming around the large paddock. The ground was softer under their feet now. The horses went "barefoot" in the winter. Heather had their shoes removed when the first snow fell. If they wore shoes in the snow, it would ball up under the frogs, or insides, of their hooves. Then they would lose their footing, as though they were on skates. A horse could be lamed if it did a "split" because of snow-clogged shoes. Cocked shoes, like the ones big Ally wore, were expensive. They had special rubber balls that fit inside his great hooves and popped the snow out. They also had "cocks," or spurs on them that dug into the ice to keep the heavy draft horse stable.

Woody saw that the maple trees on the far side of the paddock had buckets, hung on spouts driven into their trunks. He went and dipped a finger in one bucket and sucked the sap collected there. It wasn't very sweet. He knew it took hours of boiling to reduce the sap to maple syrup. He turned back to the paddock to watch the horses. He loved horses and wished he could live on this horse farm, instead of the small apartment he shared with his mom.

"These are new horses you've got, aren't they?" he asked. Ben explained that because some were new, Heather tried out the five horses by putting them together in the arena in the barn to see how they got along. They all behaved well in each other's company in the arena, so they also could be in the paddock together. He pointed out that Hendrik and Ally, the largest horses, hung out together, while Sugar followed them around. Chester and Silver were left to make a pair, which worked out well. The five horses seemed to enjoy the cool spring air outdoors.

Woody thought about learning to ride. He knew Ben could ride any of the horses, even Silver. He wondered if it would cost a lot to have riding lessons. He asked Ben.

"Well, sure," said Ben. "We have to charge for riding lessons. But I'll tell you what: When school's out, you talk to Heather about helping out here—with stalls and grooming and cleaning tack, I mean. I'll show you how to do it, and I'll bet she'll give you lessons for free."

Woody looked pleased with the idea and a little anxious. When they went inside, Ben tried out the idea on Heather. "Hey Heth, do you think Woody could do some chores here in vacation—and get riding lessons?"

Heather looked at Woody. She thought *He never gets to see his father, and Ben never gets to see his mother. They're in the same boat.* She nodded. *And so am I.*

Heather got out of bed one Saturday morning and stretched, yawning. She peered through her window to check the weather. It was less dark outside now because of daylight savings, and she could see vague forms across the drive in the paddock. Horses! All five of them in the paddock already! Who had let them out?

All the stalls in the barn had doors to the paddock outside, as well as doors that led to the indoor arena. The horses were fed and watered in their stalls every morning before the doors to the paddock were opened.

"Ben!" she called through his bedroom door, "did you let the horses out?"

Ben rolled over. He didn't open his eyes. "No," he managed to mumble before falling back to sleep.

Their dad had left the night before on a business trip, so Heather pulled on her clothes and went outside to see what was up. There was no one in the barn. There was no one in the paddock, except five horses.

Heather examined the paddock doors to the stalls. They had crossbars on the outside that fitted in metal holders to keep them shut. All the bars were slid sideways, and all the doors were open. She saw teeth marks on the bars. Heather knew who had opened them. Sugar! The smart little horse had shown before that she could open stall doors with her teeth.

She leaned against the paddock gate and shouted, "Sugar, I'm going to fix you!"

How could she make Sugar's stall teeth-proof? A large plank that had to be lifted would do it. Now where was a suitable plank? Heather went to the lumber supply, which hung on two supports from the ceiling of the garage-shed where her father kept his car.

On tiptoe, she reached up and slid a long plank out of the pile over her head. She figured a five-foot length should do it. Sugar couldn't raise that long a plank.

Heather dragged out two sawhorses and set the plank across them. She went to get the chainsaw. At that moment, she remembered her dad saying that the chainsaw was too old to be used anymore. It needed refitting. *Just one more cut—it'll hold up for one more.*

She measured the board and made a mark on it. Then she started the chainsaw motor. She leaned over the plank with it and—THWACK! The toothed chain came off the saw and whizzed into the dirt at her feet.

Heather stared at it. She knew the chain could have gone through her stomach. Or her head. Feeling a little dizzy, she stopped the motor of the saw and laid it down. She walked slowly back to the house and into the kitchen and sat down. Ben was actually out of bed.

"Breakfast?" he said cheerily.

"Uh—in a few minutes," whispered Heather. Now she was the one in trouble. When her dad saw that broken chain, she'd be in for it. Safety on the farm was Rule No. 1. After his warning, she had no excuse.

After a few minutes she got out her phone and rang Kathy. A little sympathy would help. But the phone just rang and rang.

CHAPTER FIVE

IT WAS THE NEXT Saturday – a day to clean the upstairs rooms, Heather supposed. She sat on the edge of her unmade bed. She thought about lugging the vacuum cleaner up from the basement. What she really wanted to do was fall back in bed. Her dad had been OK about the chainsaw—just said he should have had it repaired before now. But that didn't stop Heather from kicking herself mentally up and down the stairs. How could she tell Ben what to do and scold him when he didn't, if she messed things up herself?

And Kathy had spent every afternoon that week over at Chrissy's, trying to be a good friend to her. Heather had to admit Chrissy needed a friend. She seemed to shun the other kids who rode horses together, but Heather thought she was just shy. An "inferiority complex." Could it be that? At any rate, she didn't have the get-up-and-go that a person needs to handle herself and her horse. But their team-penning practice had improved, ever since Heather had found a herd of beef cows that a friendly farmer would let them practice on.

She sat and listened. The house was quiet—no sound from Ben's room. He must be still asleep. She thought about his pacemaker. No worry there—he never complained of fatigue, now, even when he came home late. Well, let him sleep. She could just enjoy a quiet morning by herself while the vacuum waited. She went out to see to the horses.

Outside it was April, a heartbreaking month in Maine. Dirty remnants of snow melted slowly to slippery ice and mud that constantly got tramped indoors. It was her job to mop and clean it up. Sometimes Heather felt sorry for herself. Other seventeen-year-old girls (like Chrissy) got to be mall-rats on Saturday, hurrying off to town to buy pretty things to wear or cosmetics. She was sure Chrissy's folks had people who cleaned their houses, and she knew they had fancy cars.

But they didn't have a Friesian horse, she reminded herself. For that matter, she had the use of the pickup, when Ben wasn't out in it, and could go off to the mall today if she chose. But she was saving her money.

Heather hated her room to be dirty and untidy. Just as she kept the horses groomed and their stalls mucked out, she also had high standards for her own quarters. Her dad helped sometimes with cleaning the kitchen and bathroom.

Only, she admitted, as she let out the horses and mucked out their stalls, when it got right down to it, she wanted her mom back with them. Never mind sharing housework, just a grownup to be there after school or in the evenings, to talk to about women's things.

But it must be worse for her dad. Heather sighed, remembering the long weeks of caring for her bed-ridden mom. Often her dad was up at night, or all day at the hospital, when the end was near. Now she headed indoors and dragged out the vac. Hauling the heavy Hoover up the stairs, she let it fall with a bump on the landing. Nothing stirred in Ben's room. Even after she ran the vacuum in her room and her dad's and then the upstairs hall, Ben slept peacefully on. She could hear him snoring softly, as she dusted around the baseboards, bedsteads, and windowsills. Finally that chore was done.

OK. I'm going to give myself a treat! Heather marched downstairs and out to the barn. Hendrik saw her coming from where he stood near the paddock fence. He put his head out over the rail. When she opened the gate, he ambled out of the paddock and stood waiting. Heather let him follow her through the barn entrance and into the big arena. She got out the big, red exercise ball. Then she climbed up the planks that railed off the corner of the arena and whistled to Hendrik. He came obediently and let her climb from the highest plank onto his back. With no saddle or stirrups, and only the rope from his halter in her hand, Heather nudged Hendrik in the ribs. He walked forward until his knees were against the red ball.

They had done this before. Hendrik pushed the ball with his forelegs until it rolled along the wall of the big indoor space. Horse and rider punted the ball all the way around the arena. Then Heather slid off, a long way to the ground and hugged Hendrik.

"Great job!" She felt better.

One day in late May, Mr. Hobbes called Heather from his office. "You'd better call Mrs. Moyer."

"What's it about, Dad?" Heather stopped brushing Hendrik and leaned her head against his warm back, while she talked on her cell phone.

"Her neighbor next door, Mrs. Lovell called me. Your pig was over there."

"Oh no! Not the neatnick with the flower garden! Was he eating her tulips?" Heather was upset. She often took riders on trails through her neighbors' property, and she was very careful to keep those neighbors happy about it. She usually checked to make sure trails were clean after horses passed. When she baked pies, she always took some to those neighbors. Now she stopped grooming Hendrik and phoned Mrs. Moyer. When the phone was answered, she got no further than, "This is Heth…"

Mrs. Moyer immediately said, "Heather? You have a pig? A pet? A pig-pet?"

"I'm so sorry, Mrs. Moyer! We try to keep him penned or indoors. Has he eaten your spring flowers?"

"Oh no. Oh, he just nibbled the tops. He didn't hurt anything."

"I was afraid he would root up your bulbs and eat them."

"No, he just rooted on the edge. I can fix that. But, boy, did he eat!"

"What did he eat?" Heather could picture Pinky Pie chewing up all the shrubbery around her neighbor's garden.

"Carrots, potatoes, bread, you name it—everything! He's so cute, I just kept feeding him!"

Oh no! Now he'll go there looking for a feast—and she won't be home, and he'll help himself to her garden!

Heather took a deep breath and thanked Mrs. Moyer for her kindness to Pinky Pie.

So Pinky Pie lost his freedom. Heather put up an electric wire about six inches above the ground. It ran around the paddock. Then she hung red flags along it, so he could see it. She put Pinky Pie in the paddock and turned on the current.

Pinky Pie noticed the wire right away. He was used to running in and out of the paddock under the wooden rails that enclosed it. He put his nose under the wire. He lifted it slightly and let it fall. Nothing happened, because the charge went around the wire every few seconds.

Then he nosed the wire up and was halfway under it when the charge hit him. Pinky Pie squealed and shot back from under the wire. Heather called him and gave him a heel of bread to chew. When he seemed comforted, she put him back in the paddock with food and water. Pinky Pie respected the wire after that. He walked nicely in and out of the paddock with Heather.

"Hey, Ben," said Heather one evening at supper. "How about the Turkey Trot? Are you going?"

"What is a Turkey Trot?" Ben wondered if it was a cowboy-style dance. "I don't think so."

Heather chuckled. "There's the 4-mile, the 6-mile, and the 8-mile. And the food is terrific!"

Ben revised his opinion. "This is riding horses?"

"You bet. I'm going to take Hendrik over for the trail riding. You could come and ride Sugar."

"You've never taken Hendrik in the trailer before."

"I know. I'm going to train him. The Turkey Trot is in two weeks. I'll sign us up."

Heather began teaching Hendrik about loading and unloading the horse trailer. First she put a small ramp on the floor of the arena. Hendrik learned to put one foot on it and then back away. Then he learned with two feet on the ramp. Soon he thought nothing of walking up the low ramp, stopping at the top, and backing down.

Finally one day, Heather led Hendrik up the steep ramp into the horse trailer. Hendrik found himself in a small, cramped space, and he didn't like it. When Heather closed the butt bar behind him, Hendrik panicked and turned around in the trailer. Then he tried to jump the butt bar.

Heather climbed into the trailer. She calmed Hendrik down. Then she turned him back around, so his hindquarters were towards the butt bar. The next two hours were spent backing Hendrik slowly down the ramp and leading him up it. It was hot and sweaty work. Every time Hendrik went up and down the ramp perfectly, Heather petted him and told him how pleased she was.

When she knew Hendrik was no longer worried by the ramp or the inside of the trailer, she gave him water and a wash down. She needed one herself!

When the day came for the Turkey Trot, Heather and Ben loaded Sugar and Hendrik into the trailer. The horses were friends. They stood quietly, side by side in the trailer. Heather drove the SUV, because Ben wasn't used to the length of the trailer. It was long and wide enough for two horses. It had bunks for camping out and a tiny washroom. It rode smoothly for the horses standing inside. It took an hour to reach the farm where the Turkey Trot was held. A crowd of people and horses was milling around in a large field. Heather paid for their tickets at the gate to the field. She knew that a large percentage of the profit made that day would go to charity. After parking the big trailer, she backed Hendrik down the ramp and praised him for doing it so nicely. She saddled him up, then led him to a spot where people were gathering before setting out on trails. Ben followed with Sugar. Hendrik attracted attention, because of his size and the way he followed Heather like a pet dog. Several people came over to learn about Friesians.

"Martha Stewart raises those horses," said one man. "They have to be flown over here, don't they?"

"Hendrik is from Holland," said Heather. "He was brought by plane when he was six months."

"Wow! Imagine a plane for a horse! Or horses!"

Heather smiled. "He was only a baby then—about 500 pounds."

"Wow!"

Heather signed herself and Ben up for the "Poker Trail." She and Ben were each handed a playing card. Ben looked at his—a queen of spades. *Please don't bring me bad luck!*

A whistle blew. The riders for the Poker Trail formed a line. A certified guide led them out of the field into a thickly wooded trail. They stayed at a walking pace until they were well spread out. Ben enjoyed riding Sugar through leafy woods after all the snow and ice of the winter was gone. Up ahead, Heather was chatting with a tall rider, as they walked their horses side by side.

Soon they began to trot, and, not long after that, they reached the first stop. Everyone crowded their horses around a small hut with a table in front where more cards were handed out. Ben saw that his new card was another queen. *That has to be good—a pair of queens!*

The group of riders continued on the scenic trail for three more stops. Sometimes they passed through open fields, and other times the trail was dark and shaded. At each place where they stopped, they received another card. Ben was excited at the last stop. His hand of cards held three queens and two tens—a full house! He looked for Heather to show her what he had, but she was deep in conversation with the young man she had been riding with.

When they returned to the farm, each person showed their cards. Heather's eyes opened wide when she saw Ben win the Poker Trail with his full house.

"Good going!" she exclaimed. She turned to her companion, "Matt, this is my brother, Ben. He helps out a lot with our string of horses."

Ben shook hands with Matt. He had to look way up into a pair of friendly brown eyes.

"Hello," he said a little shyly.

"Congratulations," said Matt. "What did you win?"

"I don't know yet. I hope it's money—I'm saving for a car."

"Probably is. They'll award prizes at dinner."

The food was set out. All kinds of meat, salads, breads, casseroles, beer and soft drinks filled the row of tables where everyone could help themselves. Best of all, to Ben's taste, were the many desserts, from pies with ice cream to mountainous cakes heaped with frosting.

While Ben was stuffing himself full, the prizes were announced. His mouth was crammed with cake when he heard his name called. Wiping his face hastily, he went forward and received an envelope. His 'thank you' sounded rather thick, but his handshake was hearty. The man handing out prizes grinned. "Food's good, isn't it?" Ben could only nod. He jammed the envelope in his pocket and hurried back to his seat.

When it was time to reload the horses and start for home, both Hendrik and Sugar went smoothly into their stalls in the trailer. Heather got into the driver's seat. She pulled out a tissue and handed it to Ben.

"Most of that cake you stuffed yourself with is on your face. I'll give you a bath when we get home—with the hose!"

Ben scrubbed at his mouth, which saved him the trouble of answering her.

"Matt is going to come over to our place and teach a group class on advanced training," she went on. "He's well known for training horses. I could learn a lot, and so could you. We'll advertise and charge admission so I can pay him. Wish I had won that prize you got!"

Heather suddenly noticed that the SUV was low on gas. She began looking for a gas station that was large enough to pull the long trailer in by the pumps and out on the road again. Finally she saw one and carefully pulled in to pump gas. Ben got out and was fueling the car, when a voice greeted him by name. It was Matt, who had pulled into the next row of pumps. After hailing Ben, he walked over to talk to Heather.

Heather was a little flustered when they said goodbye. She waved at Matt as she swung the SUV out of the gas station. She left enough room for a wide swing so the trailer would clear the entryway but failed to notice a tall lamppost near the road. The horse trailer crunched against the post.

Biting her lip, Heather jumped out of the truck and rushed to snatch open the trailer door and check the horses. Both Hendrik and Sugar were on their feet, their heads turned toward her with curiosity written on their faces.

"Thank Goodness!" Heather leaned her head against the trailer. She felt weak with relief. But she saw the back of the trailer was badly dented.

"Too bad."

Her cheeks reddened when she turned her head and saw Matt standing next to her, gravely regarding the damage.

"Your undercarriage is all right," he went on, "you should make it home with no problem. I gather the horses are up?"

"Yes." Blushing hotly, Heather said goodbye to him again. She drove Ben home without saying a word. Ben felt sorry for her. He also felt a little glad that he wasn't the only one to mess up! And he had a new hundred dollar bill in his pocket!

Heather tried to make up her mind. Should she? Shouldn't she? She asked Kathy, while they drove home from school. "Do you think I should ask Matt to be my date for the prom?"

Kathy was silent a moment. Then she gave Heather an affectionate push. "Of course!"

"I don't really know him that well yet. And he's out of high school, doing training. Would he come?"

"You can only try, my dear. Me, I'm counting on good old George." They both laughed. George was Kathy's cousin and good friend. It wouldn't be a romantic date, but Kathy and her cousin would have fun.

As it turned out, Matt did accept Heather's invitation. The evening of the prom, she discarded her usual jeans for a strapless dress and shawl. Kathy hung on George's arm, wearing a blouse and long skirt that could have been her mother's. Matt turned up with a sedan, and they all crowded in. The school auditorium was decorated with signs congratulating the senior class, but they could hardly be seen for the crowd on the dance floor. Heather found Matt to be a good dancer and complimented him. He laughed and told her he went for a job at a dance studio one summer. He thought he would be sweeping cigarette butts, but they grabbed him and said, "let us show you our routine!" So he wound up teaching ballroom as well as jazz dancing.

Kathy was twirling with George, her head thrown back and laughing. Soon she was asked to dance by other partners, and even Matt took her out on the floor.

"Wow," she said later to Heather, "you picked a great dancer!"

"A surprise," Heather admitted. "And I like him. But, you know, Kathy, I mostly admire him for his horsemanship. He's agreed to do a training event at our place. Wait 'til you see him juggle a tribe of nervous nellies."

Kathy rather thought she would like to see that.

When the last weeks of June rolled around, school was out at last. A large number of snow days had made the school year last longer than usual. Everyone was ready for summer plans.

Team-penning practice was going well. Horses and riders enjoyed their practice, both with oil cans and with real cows. They timed themselves and were pleased with the results. "Gosh!" Kathy said, "We're becoming experts!" They were walking across the stable yard toward the Hobbes' house for refreshments, Kathy between Heather and Chrissy. She put her arms around their shoulders and hugged them. "We'll do better this time!"

Kathy's enthusiasm always lightened the mood of any group she was in. Chrissy responded with a smile, and Heather felt a sense of security, as she hugged Kathy back. The three of them were friends now, and their teamwork showed it.

Ben stood in front of the full-length mirror in the family bathroom and inspected his body. Last year his legs had grown longer and stronger, but his chest and arms were puny. He thought maybe he was filling out a little. Now that he was allowed to carry wood, it was paying off in larger biceps. Maybe, if he lifted weights at the gym, his pecs would get bigger, too. Woody was chunky with strong arms. He always won when they Indian-wrestled. But Ben was taller. He flexed one of his arms experimentally. Yep, definitely larger.

At lunch he had a question for his father: "Dad, could I get a membership at the health club?"

His father looked at him. "You could if you earn it. You thought yet about a summer job?"

Ben's eyebrows were raised, his blue eyes reflective. A job. This was a new idea.

"What kind of job could I get?"

"You've got a driver's license. There's a new restaurant in town—serves Asian food. Bet they could use someone to deliver for them, now the tourists are arriving."

"You mean, use the pickup?"

"No, they've probably got a car. You could give it a try."

Ben thought it over. Then he got dressed in his best summer clothes and drove the pickup to the Thai-Asian restaurant. The manager looked Ben over and asked about his driving record.

"It's good," Ben assured him. "I'm very careful—the trooper who gave me my license even said so."

The manager looked at the license Ben showed him. "I suppose this would be just for the summer?"

"And after school in the fall," Ben said quickly. "I won't go out for sports until baseball starts."

"We'll give it a try," said the manager, to Ben's delight. Feeling elated, he drove home, trying to keep his foot from weighing down the gas pedal. He exploded into the house.

"I did it! I got a job!"

His father looked up from the newspaper. "I know. The owner of the place called me to check you out. I told him you were young but careful. Keep it that way."

"I will!" Ben was emphatic.

Heather came to the door of the kitchen, a dishcloth in her hand. Ben would need the pickup to get to the car at his job. When their dad was away, that would leave her high and dry, with no wheels, unless she dropped him off every day. *But maybe they'll fill him up with their noodles and stuff, and I won't have to feed him so much!*

But she needed the pickup now to fetch her cap and gown from school. Graduation day was coming up, and life was getting exciting! She prayed for good weather, which would mean a graduation ceremony outside on the school lawn, rather than in the auditorium.

When the day came, she marched in full regalia at the head of her class, carrying a tasseled staff. Kathy marched next to her, with a similar staff. They split off as they neared the stage where the principal of the school and other dignitaries sat and held their staffs on the ground at each row as their classmates filed into their seats.

What a day! She could see her dad taking pictures and Ben standing on his seat to see. When her name was called, she mounted the steps to the stage, holding her gown up carefully and accepted her diploma as her friends cheered. A big feast followed the ceremony at a local restaurant. Her dad, along with other parents, made sure everyone ordered what they wanted. Kathy's dad came, but her mother was absent. Heather wondered what that meant.

CHAPTER SIX

ON THE DAY IN July when Matt came to demonstrate advanced training, Heather got up early. Even so, her dad was up before her. He was out in the shed, rummaging in the storage area. When Heather joined him, he showed her the old deck chairs he had found. "If you're serving lunch, people will want to sit," he said. Just then Kathy rode in on Tess. She tethered the gray horse to the paddock fence and came to help.

Together she and Heather carried the deck chairs over near the long picnic table in the side yard and set them up. Twenty-five people had signed up to learn from Matt. Some of them would bring their own horses. By eleven o'clock, she and Kathy had made sixty lobster rolls and a huge salad. Bottles of soda and beer were packed in ice in a cooler. Kathy said she hoped Chrissy would come and bring Silver. That horse could use some training!

Woody was also there early to help get stalls cleaned and horses fed and watered. He worked with Mr. Hobbes, wondering where Ben was. Towards nine, just as trucks with trailers began to pull in, Ben showed up in the barn, looking sheepish. Overslept, he said. Heather wore a frown, but her father just went on welcoming those who had come. By 10 o'clock, everyone had arrived, there was a line of vehicles parked off the drive, and the visiting horses were spaced along one side of the arena in the barn, tied to the wall. Heather was pleased to see Chrissy's SUV and trailer come up the drive. She hallooed and waved to her. Chrissy looked a little sunburned but wore an air of confidence.

Matt came a little after everyone else. He was wearing old jeans and a plaid flannel shirt. His dark hair was ruffled. He ran his hand over it, as he led a short, brown and white mare toward the barn. Heather went to meet him. He smiled at her but motioned her away from the mare.

"This here's Ruff," he said, "short for Roughneck, I guess. She doesn't much like the trailer, but I thought she'd make a good demo."

"She's welcome, and so are you," Heather smiled back. She went toward the barn, intending to make a wide path for Matt and Ruff. Matt called her back.

"How about I start in the paddock with lunging? That'll get the fidgets out of her, maybe."

"Sure thing." Heather continued into the barn to move the group out to the paddock. When they were all watching from the rails, Matt addressed the crowd.

"Hello, everyone and thanks for coming. I'm going to start this class with lunging. My friend Ruff here will help. She's an Icelandic horse. You can see she has small feet. She can go fast, her ride is smooth, and, small as she is, she can carry a big man. I'm going to teach her about personal space, using this long lunge line. These things here on the end of the line are "poppers." If Ruff crowds me, I'll slap her rump with them. Also, watch what I do if she pays attention to anybody but me."

Matt clicked his tongue at Ruff. He stood in the center of the paddock and encouraged Ruff, until she was trotting in a wide circle around him, attached to the lunge line. If Ruff veered toward him, he swung the poppers on her rump. The noise bothered her enough so she quickly returned to the length of the rope.

Every once in a while, Matt let her stand still to rest. She looked at him then to see what he wanted. Once, she turned her head away to survey the crowd at the rail. At once, Matt made her run again and kept her running each time she failed to attend to him. Finally, her behavior was perfect, and she looked only at him while standing still. Matt walked to her then, fondled her neck, and gave her a lump of sugar. "Good job, Ruff!" he said in a pleased tone. Ruff put her ears forward and whinnied.

When the class returned to the arena, Matt tied Ruff to a space along the wall, not far from the other horses. He asked the crowd if anyone had brought a troublesome horse. A woman raised her hand.

"Maribel, here, she's stubborn as a mule – won't do anything I ask."

Matt untied Maribel from her place at the wall and attached the lunge line. Picking up a manure fork with one hand, he ran Maribel back and forth the length of the arena. If she even slowed down, he raised the fork in a threatening manner, which caused her to leap forward again. He kept this up until she was huffing. Then he walked toward her, not looking in her eyes, and took hold of her halter. He led the exhausted horse to tie her to the wall again but stopped every few feet to show who was in charge, while the class applauded, and Stephanie, Maribel's owner, looked pleased.

"Anyone else?" he asked.

Chrissy raised her hand tentatively. Matt saw her and walked over to her. "What can I do for you, young lady?"

Chrissy's cheeks were pink. "I have this horse, the white one," she pointed at Silver. "She's just so nervous and fidgety."

"Let's see you get on her." Chrissy hesitated, then hurried over to Silver.

"Just a moment." Matt's voice was kind. "If you've got a fidgety horse, you walk up to her real slow. Slow walk, slow voice, everything quiet, so she knows she's safe. Come back here and approach her again."

This time Chrissy walked slowly but deliberately to her horse. She spoke slowly to Silver, keeping her voice low. When she mounted, as slowly as she could, Silver stayed quiet, waiting for her to settle in the saddle. Chrissy looked surprised. "She always shied before, when I got on." Matt chuckled. "Now you know the secret. Let's see you walk her."

With more assurance, Chrissy gave Silver the signal to move forward a step. Then she backed her a step and turned her left, trotting in place. Matt clapped his hands softly, seeing how Chrissy was training Silver in dressage. "Good going," he said quietly. Chrissy dismounted, blushing at the nods and thumbs-up she saw in the crowd that was watching.

Matt began telling the class about horse blankets—how horses only need a shelter outside to move under if they choose. Putting coats or horse blankets on them when they're outside makes them sweat, he said. The sweat turns to ice. So, with coats, they get hot then cold—and then they catch cold.

While Matt was talking, Ben took the opportunity to run a wheelbarrow behind the row of tied horses and shovel up manure they had let drop. When he passed behind Ruff, she showed her nervous nature by panicking. She kicked out at Ben, then reared, tearing a plank from the barn wall. The plank frightened her still more, and she flailed around with it. Ben ducked back, but when Heather moved forward, the plank struck her on the arm.

Matt walked over to detach the plank. He led the shuddering horse before the crowd. "Watch how I desensitize her." He spent the next ten minutes rubbing Ruff all over with the loose plank, until she was used to it and remained calm. Then he tied her to the wall and spent another ten minutes running a wheelbarrow back and forth behind her, while talking to the class.

"I'm doing this for her and me both," he told them. "She's going to a new owner in a month or so, when we've got the fidgets worked out. When she's got so she's under control, we'll start dressage. She should be good at it, with her little feet and sensitivity to command. She may be scared now, but she's no dummy."

When the class was over, Matt came to Heather, looking anxious. "How's your arm? Nothing serious, I hope?"

Heather rubbed her upper arm self-consciously. "It'll be OK. I'll just look black and blue in a bathing suit."

"I'd like to see that!" he grinned at her. Heather remembered her duties as hostess.

"Lunch on the lawn, everyone!" she called, hurrying to the kitchen. Kathy and Chrissy helped her carry out platters of lobster rolls and the big salad bowl. Soon the class of horse owners sat around the picnic tables under shady maple trees with their cool drinks and lunches. They were enthusiastic about Matt's class.

"Really worth it," said Stephanie. "Now I know how I can make Maribel go like a dream."

"I'd like to see him teach dressage," said another woman. "He's neat."

Heather walked around the yard, passing out seconds on lobster rolls, while Kathy cut up watermelons into slices. She noticed a pickup truck pulling up next to the barn.

"I better see who that is," she said, handing the platter to Ben, who took it eagerly. Heather was surprised to see a familiar face rise out of the pickup, one she hadn't seen for months, though they had sent each other a lot of texts and Facebook messages.

"Russ!" she exclaimed.

"Hi Heather!" The tall, redheaded young man with a cheerful smile came toward her. "You got a party going on?" He gestured at the group around the picnic table.

"It's an equine class. Sorry, you've missed the training."

"No problem," he grinned. "I came to see if you'd like a lift to the Equine Fair next month?"

"Well," Heather was a little flustered. "I don't know yet if I'm going. I mean, I want to," she added hastily, seeing his face fall, "but I have to ask—to earn—I mean, the arrangements aren't made yet!"

"Could I be an arrangement?" He looked at her hopefully.

"Sure thing." Heather got herself together. "I'll have to let you know. Maybe after my birthday. My dad usually gives me something ..."

"How old will you be?"

"Eighteen," she replied, just as Matt joined them. "Uh, this is Matt, our trainer. Matt, this is Russ. He drives a Clydesdale." The young men shook hands.

"You got a big horse," Matt said conversationally to Russ.

"Yep," said Russ. He stuck his hands in his jeans pockets. Matt draped an arm over Heather's shoulder.

"Heather, here, has a stableful," said Matt, "come and take a look."

"I got to get moving." Russ smiled at them both. He whispered to Heather, "Text me, OK?"

He hopped into his truck, turned it around, and was off down the drive. Matt looked sideways at Heather. "Got a date?"

Heather shrugged. "Maybe the Fair. I don't know yet"

"The Equine Fair? Wish I weren't heading west."

"Where are you going? Not moving away?" Heather hoped this horse expert would stick around her neighborhood.

"No. I've got a training job in Nevada next month. Sure hate to miss the Fair, though."

Heather murmured in sympathy. She turned to see people rising to put their paper plates in the trashcan. She went to help tidy up. Later, when the horse trailers were reloaded and Heather had signed up several owners to go trail riding, she came face to face with Ben.

"How much did we make?" he asked eagerly.

"Who's WE," she snapped. "You ran out on me, you rat! Maybe you thought you were a guest, showing up when everyone was here! I made some money on this, all right, but, believe me, not much goes to you!"

"OK, OK, Heather!" Ben held his elbow in front of his face, as though expecting a blow. "I know I goofed off. Woody helped Dad out, didn't he? And I get some credit for bringing Woody on."

From Heather's face, it didn't look like she was giving him credit for anything, he thought. Best to scuttle like a bug before she stepped on him. His sister usually cooled off overnight.

Heather drew breath to tell him what she thought of him, but let it go, as he walked away. She had a good amount of admission fees, and, anyway, Ben had worked in the barn with the guest horses. She had something else to think about, anyway. *Did I really stand there by the barn, talking to two good-looking men, one of them asking me to ride with him to the Fair? That's a nice thought to take to bed tonight!*

Chapter Seven

The August sun was setting as Ben found the address where he was to deliver his last bag of boxes filled with Pad Thai and spring rolls. The air was still hot, so he held the warm bag away from his body as he walked up the flagstone path to the front steps of the large house. He stood on the terraced porch and rang the doorbell.

When the door opened, a pretty girl about his age appeared. Her mouth opened in an "O" before she smiled at him. "Oh, thank you! Just a minute, I'll get the check." She set the bag on a table and held the door wider. "Come in and get cool!"

Ben looked after her, wondering why she seemed familiar. While he waited, he stood near the air conditioner and enjoyed the cool breeze on his hot arms. He could feel the sweat running down his back. That was the only trouble with the Thai-Asian car—no AC. But you only need it in Maine for two months, anyway.

When the girl brought him a check and started to open the door for him, he said, "Wait, don't I know you from somewhere? Maybe high school?"

She shook her head shyly. "No. You just saw me one time. I go to a private school."

"Really? When did I see you? What's your name? Besides Stewart," he added, looking at the check.

"It's Susan." She looked even shyer. "I owe you a lot for what you did."

Ben was baffled. "What? When?"

"It was on the Interstate. Last fall. I had an accident with a deer." Susan peeped up at him and whispered, "I've always wanted to thank you."

Ben slapped his forehead. "A deer—of course I remember you!" He leaned casually against the doorframe. "So, Susan. I'll tell you how to thank me." He looked down into her face. "Would you take in a movie with me?"

He waited. Then, shy still, she nodded.

Heather considered her eighteenth birthday a success. She lined up her cards on the breakfast table. A heart on the one from Russ. She had agreed to go to the Equine Fair with him. Ben's was a funny one, with a horse informing her behind his hoof that the birthday wishes came "straight from the horse's mouth!" Matt's mailing of the brochure for his training class in Nevada had come the day before. Just by accident, she thought, but she lined it up with the birthday cards. Best of all, her dad's card included a couple of hundred dollar bills.

"Oh Dad!" She had thrown her arms around his neck. "I'll have a ball at the Fair!"

"I know you're responsible," he hugged her back.

Ben joked, "Don't lay it all on one horse!" He watched while she unwrapped his gift. She took a red bandana out of the box and then, when she opened it, a ticket to the Fair dropped out.

"Oh Ben!" She hugged him hard.

"I sent for it," said Ben modestly. "I thought it wouldn't come in time, but it was in the mail yesterday."

"I wondered why you were racing down the drive to the mailbox," laughed Heather. "I thought you were getting more pec-building ads, but now I know!" When Ben blushed, she added, "Wish you could go too, Ben."

"I'm a working man," said Ben, cheerfully, "and, boy, does my car smell good!" Heather knew Ben had learned to love Asian cuisine, since the manager of the restaurant gave him boxes of extra food to take home. Seems the manager was fond of her little brother—now not so little, either.

A few days later, she went to the paddock to say goodbye to the horses. They all came to the rail when they saw her. She pressed her face into Hendrik's mane. "I'll be back soon," she whispered in his ear. "Kathy and Woody will take care of you."

He answered her with a whicker, that special sound horses make for those they know and like to be with. Heather told Sugar to take care of herself and not do anything silly. Then she gave Ally a hug and a pat. She made sure all the horses had water in the trough in the paddock—it was an old claw-footed bathtub.

"Goodbye," she called to them all. She went back to the house to collect her knapsack. When she came out with it, a small pig was yipping and squealing and poking his nose under the paddock gate.

"Pinky Pie! How could I forget you!" She found the bag of old bread scraps in the barn and fed him a few. Pinky Pie gobbled them up. He put one small hoof on the lowest bar of the gate and looked up at Heather. He made small yips and whines.

"No, you stay there with your friends. I'll see you in three days." Heather shouldered her pack and leaned against the gate. It was time to meet Russ. They had agreed on the phone that she would pay for gas, and she had the money ready. When his red pickup came swerving around the bend in the drive, Heather gave the horses and pig one last look and went to meet Russ. He leaned over and opened the door.

"Hi, Heather! Come on—I want you to know I cleaned up the passenger seat for you!" Russ's red hair curled wildly. His blue eyes looked excited. Heather gave him a smile in answer and climbed in. Both her dad and Ben were away at work, so she just waved goodbye to Hendrik and Pinkie Pie.

The ride to Springfield was a long one. Heather and Russ both liked the same radio station and sang along with the songs. Russ told Heather about his veterinary studies. "I've been helping deliver calves. It takes all you've got for strength when you have to reach inside the cow."

Heather was fascinated to learn about veterinary skills and asked many questions. It seemed a short while later they were in Springfield. When they had parked the pickup in a big field with other cars, Heather got out and looked around. There were several big tents to be seen in the fairgrounds that lay next to the parking lot. She and Russ headed for the admissions gate, where Heather gave up the ticket Ben had given her, and Russ reached for his wallet.

"Here's the gas money." Heather handed him twenty dollars, and they passed into the fairgrounds. A big crowd was milling around the tents. "Thousands of people," Heather guessed out loud, and Russ agreed, looking around. They walked through the nearest tent, inspecting the booths on either side.

Everything that involved horses or riding was there: books, tapes, tack, saddles, wearing apparel (for rider and horse), harnesses, masks and netting for protection against insects, portable fencing, even manure forks. One of the booths was occupied by a famous equestrian. He looked just as she had seen him on TV, with a big head of gray hair and a gray mustache. She whispered his name to Russ and pointed.

They walked over to the man's booth—Frank MacLean was his name. He noticed Heather and smiled at her. Then, to her amazement, he left the people who were looking at his pictures and tapes and spoke to her!

"Aren't you one of the girls who competed in the team penning event at Farmington?" he asked.

There was some color in Heather's cheeks, as she nodded. Russ was looking at her with surprised admiration.

"I was there. I saw you," Frank MacLean went on, "Some pizzazz you got, competing with those pros!"

Heather returned his smile. "I guess we need more practice. But we've been working on it!"

"Just so. It looked to me like you could put up a good show another time."

Heather was now quite pink. People were turning to look. "Thank you" she managed to say, before Frank turned back to his customers. She peeked at Russ as they walked on.

"Say, you really are something!" he murmured. Heather hurried to change the subject before her face turned bright crimson. "Let's go to the demo tent!"

"OK," Russ was agreeable. In the demo tent they found a big sawdust ring where a woman was demonstrating dressage. To Heather's amazement, the woman was riding a mule! She and Russ watched intently as the large mule performed piaffe, trotting in place, and then rotated on his hind legs during a canter, as directed by his rider. He lifted his hooves as daintily as any well-trained horse.

Heather whispered to Russ, "I wonder if I could train Ali for dressage. He's a sport horse, big and sure-footed." Russ nodded. He waited until the audience clapped for the mule and rider who finished their pattern and remained immobile.

Then he said, "You'd need to buy an English saddle, wouldn't you, and wear chaps to keep your legs from being pinched in the saddle leathers?"

"Well, there's cowboy dressage, too," answered Heather. "Anyway, I've got chaps for team penning." She wondered if

Matt could advise her about dressage and decided to ask him when he returned.

The next person in the sawdust ring was a man talking about biomechanics—the movement of the rider's body with the horse. They decided to walk further and found a row of gigs. They were light-wheeled carriages with tiny seats and long shafts on which drivers had to balance with their heels out in front of them in harness races.

"Have you ever ridden one of those?" Heather asked Russ.

"I've tried," he said, looking rueful.

Heather laughed. "You don't sound enthusiastic. Where did you race?"

"I didn't race. Just tried to get around the track. Harness racers really get the pace up!"

"But where was the track?" Heather persisted.

Russ shrugged. "Friend of my father's. A big place. Enough said."

Heather was left with more questions, but they were now in front of a snack stand. She bought a corn dog and enjoyed eating it from the top down, as it cooled. Russ's choice was a hearty piece of fried dough, heavy with oil and powdered sugar.

"That should fill you up!" Heather waved her corn dog to cool it. "What shall we do next?"

"I'd like to see Frank MacLean's show," answered Russ.

"So would I!"

"The sign on his booth said two pm."

Heather consulted her watch. "That's in, um, twenty minutes."

"OK. But I have to meet someone at three, OK? We could split up then and meet again for supper."

Heather was surprised but tried not to show it. "Ok with me."

Still munching as they walked through the fairgrounds, they paused by a shop selling cowboy boots. Heather thought most of them too flashy with their white stripes and glassy gems. "I'd rather spend my money on dressy chaps," she said. "My brown leathers get soiled from holding up hooves to pick stones out. Maybe I'll shop for some while you're—busy."

"Look, it's just ... well, never mind." It was Russ's turn to turn a little pink. "Let's hit MacLean's show."

Frank MacLean gave an excellent demonstration of cowboy-style riding in the largest tent. He was in and out of the saddle on both sides of his white horse while it galloped. He used a lasso, whirling the noose over his head before letting it go to settle under the scampering legs of a calf. Then he sprang off his horse and quickly bound all four legs until the calf lay motionless on the ground.

While he was off the horse, he showed how he could use whistles and hand signals to make it bow, walk on its hind legs, and lie down dead. The applause from the audience was loud after each demonstration.

Heather forgot the time, until Russ whispered in her ear, "Got to go now. I'll see you at the Equine Café at six. OK, Heather?"

She nodded, and he slipped down from the stands where they were sitting. Where was he going? To see who? Whom, she corrected herself. They weren't really on a date. He just offered her a ride. She didn't even know where he was lodging for two nights.

She gave up thinking about it and watched Frank MacLean take his white horse through a complicated dressage routine. She noticed his jeweled saddle had a horn. So that must be cowboy dressage.

After the show, Heather went looking for a booth that sold chaps. When she found one, it was crowded with people looking through a colorful assortment of leather goods—belts, hats, vests, skirts, even dresses, as well as chaps. She squeezed past a chunky woman who was picking through gaucho outfits and holding them up against herself. The next table had kerchiefs and wide belts with fancy buckles.

Finally, she found a rack of chaps. A white pair, studded with silver stars caught her eye. She pulled them from the rack and consulted the tag. Pricey, but within her budget, thanks to Dad's generosity and the money saved by Ben's ticket. She tried them on, buckling the straps around the legs of her jeans. They were perfect! Also, flashy, she admitted to herself. Never mind, they would match the white hat she wore for team penning.

She paid for them and wandered on among the booths. One was on horse dentistry. Another was on horse diseases. Listening to the expert who was speaking, Heather learned that Friesian horses are considered "drafty," because they are heavy, and that drafty horses can easily get colic. Also, they have to be watched for black water. This disease was known as "Monday sickness," because Sunday used to be the day off for draft horses, and the toxins in their kidneys appeared on Mondays. Heather left the booth, vowing to watch Hendrik for colic and black water.

There seemed to be a crowd gathering on the big lawn at the center of the fairgrounds. Some people were seated, as though they were waiting for something to happen. She asked a woman in a folding chair, "What's going on?" The woman answered in a broad Maine accent, "The govnah's agoin' tah speak."

The governor—no wonder there's a crowd! Heather was curious to see the governor of the state. She was now of voting age and should take more interest in elected officials. She found an unused chair nearby and pulled it up. The woman smiled at her and asked, "Where's you frum?"

"China," Heather told her. "You?"

"We come down by t'bus last night frum Machias. Porcupine eat the tires off'n th' pickup and no time to buy new."

Heather exclaimed in sympathy, and the woman offered her a soiled bag of chips, that she politely refused.

She noticed a raised platform a little way off. As they waited, a small group of people gathered by the platform. Eventually, five or six of them climbed the stairs and seated themselves at the back. A microphone stood in front, where someone would announce the governor.

At last he mounted the platform. There were two men with him, one of them looked quite young. Heather screwed up her eyes—*It couldn't be ... it looks like—Russ!*

The other man seized the microphone and asked everyone to stand and welcome the governor of this great state. A roar of greeting and applause went up. The governor was an impressively large man with a shock of white hair. He waved to the crowd, then took the microphone and began to speak. He said how glad he was to see everyone and wasn't it a great day for the Equine Fair? There was more applause.

Heather watched Russ standing near the governor. She wondered what he was doing up there. Maybe he was security or something. Did he lie about becoming a vet?

Some people were dragging chairs in front of Heather, so she had to excuse herself and pull her feet back. When she looked back at the platform, people were applauding, and Russ had taken the last empty chair on the podium. She thought *What is going on? Will he still meet me at the Café? Who and what are you, Russ? You'll have some explaining to do!*

When the governor's speech on the economics and popularity of his state was over, Heather's watch told her she had ten minutes to meet Russ. She walked to the Café and got an outside table. She scanned the crowd streaming by but couldn't see Russ. Was he going to stand her up? She ordered a beverage and began to think she would be eating alone.

A knot of people talking among themselves came slowly along. Russ was right behind them. He jumped the small fence around the tables and fell into the chair opposite her.

"Heather!" he said, his eyes shining.

"Russ!" said Heather, matching his tone. "What goes on? Why were you up on the stand with the governor?"

"Well, he's ... you see," Russ appeared embarrassed but finally got the words out, "He's my father."

Heather sat in stunned silence. Then she looked Russ in the eye. "And I'm not good enough to meet him."

"No!" Russ shouted. "I mean, yes! He's coming here to meet you!"

When Heather just sat with her mouth open, Russ went on, "I'll be quick—he'll be here any minute. He didn't like it much when I chose vet school. He wanted me to be a doctor. So I left and took that summer job on Mt. Desert, where I met you. Now he's so glad I'm back, I can go to any school I want. But I wasn't sure, Heather. I had to talk to him alone, and that takes time and arguing with people about his schedule. Oh, Heather, here he is!"

And Heather was suddenly shaking hand with the tall, white-haired man that she knew was the governor.

"Of course you'll stay with us," he was saying. "Russ, bring this lovely young lady along to the hotel so I can get to know her!" Then he was gone, surrounded by reporters asking questions.

There was a pause. Heather's legs felt shaky, so she sat down. So did Russ. "Now that's over, how about a Maine lobster?" He smiled at her, his eyes twinkling, and picked up the menu.

CHAPTER EIGHT

HEATHER CALLED HOME FROM the hotel. "Hey, Dad, how's it going? Good. Well you'd never guess where I've got to." After she told him, she could hear exclamations in the background. Then Ben got on the phone extension. "You're *where*? You mean that guy who drove the sleigh for our class trip was our governor's son? Cool!"

"Very cool," Heather assured him. "You should see the room I'm staying in! I thought I'd be at some ABC motel in the burbs, but this is the finest the state has to offer!"

"Heather," her dad's voice sounded strained. "I know you're of age, but are you safe? Have you got your doors double-locked—right now, I mean?"

"It's OK, Dad. The hallway is paved with security guards anyway—no one could possible get in!" Heather laughed. "I'll tell you every detail when I'm home again. But, yeah, I'm safe."

"Matt called you," her dad said.

Heather snapped back to reality. "Where is he?"

"Somewhere out west. Said he was just calling to chat about horses. Horses." Her dad sounded exasperated. "Sometimes I wonder ..."

Heather laughed again. "I've got plans for him. Ever heard of cowboy dressage, Dad?"

"No, and it sounds like work. I've got my own, so, if you're sure everything's OK?"

"I'm one hundred percent OK!"

Ben coaxed Susan to go horseback riding with him on a trail. Her first lesson in the paddock had gone well. Big Ally was slow and gentle and never spooked at anything. Woody had joined her, on Sugar. He had begun lessons in the summer and could trot and canter now.

"C'mon with us!" Ben urged. "Ally will keep you safe, and you're used to him now. Matt and Heather are going too, and Chrissy will ride her mare, Silver. I'll be on Sugar, and Woody can ride Chester."

Susan finally agreed. On the afternoon of the trail ride, she watched Ben saddle up Sugar.

"She'll puff herself up when you fasten the girth," Ben told her, as he pulled the cinch tight under Sugar's belly. "All you have to do is wait until she has to take another breath and then yank it tight." Sugar danced sideways in the opening to the barn, where she was tied to a ring in the wall. Susan admired the way Ben followed the horse, crowding her and adjusting the saddle leathers.

"Doesn't it hurt? Can't you leave it loose?"

"If I let her get away with faking a tight girth, it would loosen on the trail, and I'd be on the ground in no time." He led Sugar out of the barn to where Ally, already saddled and bridled, stood by the mounting block. Holding Sugar's reins with one hand, he helped steady Susan on the block, as she got one foot in a stirrup and swung the other over Ally's back.

Susan felt high up in the air on Ally's back, but when they walked their horses to join Heather, Chrissy, Woody, and Matt, she saw that Heather was just as high on Hendrik. Heather sat the big Friesian with her back straight. Her legs didn't reach very far down his big sides, but she kept her heels down and toes pointed forward. Her wide white hat was snug over her brown curls.

Hendrik was now grown to full size for a Friesian. He weighed 1500 pounds and stood 16.3 hands at the shoulder. He was now used to having a rider and saddle on his back. He had learned proper etiquette in the arena and on the trails.

Which was a good thing, because Matt was leading the group, and Heather wanted Hendrik to make a good impression. When the group of six was gathered and ready, she nudged Hendrik to move into a walk and led the group across the field to where the trail began, as a narrow path, leading into deep woods.

Matt entered the trail first on the roan horse he brought in his trailer. Chrissy moved to follow him with Silver, then Ben on Sugar. Susan came next after Ben, and Heather brought up the rear on Hendrik, with Woody on Chester, to keep an eye on Susan. But she knew Ally would amble quietly with Susan, keeping his nose near Sugar's tail, and, of course, Sugar liked Ally and Hendrik to follow her.

It was lovely to be out on a trail in early September. The trail was a tunnel through leafy trees, their branches casting deep, cool shade on the riders. The clop of the horses' hooves was a comfortable sound, muffled, but steady on the sandy path. There would be bridges and streams to cross. Heather knew the trail well. It wound up and down through the hills that backed the Hobbes' horse farm. She had explained to Matt which forks to take that would bring them back home after a good ride.

Heather enjoyed the glimpses of color where the leaves of the maple trees were starting to turn red and yellow in contrast to the evergreen trees. Maine is the pine tree state, she thought, reining Hendrik back a little to give Ally space. Maine has the bright maples like Vermont and New Hampshire, but we have the green pines too, so we have color all year!

She saw that Ben was turning often to check out how Susan was doing. The girl seemed more confident now. When the trail widened, Heather rode up beside Susan and Ally.

"How's it going?"

"I'm OK," Susan said, "I like this, it's great!"

"Your horse likes it too. You're a featherweight for Ally. I know a woman who must be 300 pounds. Her horse really works! And she keeps him outdoors all year with only a lean-to for shelter."

"That's cruel!"

"Yes. The shelter only has three sides and a tarp over the top. She's looking for trouble, especially with her weight and the way the snowmobile riders tear up the wooden bridges. I hope the animal warden catches up with her."

Ben thought he should be riding next to Susan. He slowed Sugar down until her tail was in Hendrik's nose.

"Hi there!" he said to Susan, ignoring Heather. "This is fun, isn't it?"

Heather tried not to laugh. She reined Hendrik back and rode with Woody. The four horses fell well behind the first two. The trail was heading downhill to a stream that the horses had to wade through. A man was working on the trail there, clearing away branches and loose stones. He wore rubber boots and held a short log in his hands, swinging it over to place it as a foothold in the stream.

That looked threatening to Silver, Chrissy's mare. She reared and sidled, rolling her eyes in fright. Chrissy used the reins to try to force her head down. She spoke quietly to her. Silver backed off the trail into the woods, and a branch caught Chrissy's shoulder. She toppled off Silver, landing with a grunt of pain on the ground. Her helmet came off and rolled under a bush.

Matt had crossed the stream already. He turned his horse when he heard the ruckus. The other riders were not yet in sight. He cantered back through the water to catch the bridle of the riderless horse. He dismounted and calmed Silver, stroking her and talking to her, until she could safely be tied to a tree. Ben, Susan, Woody, and Heather came into view and held their horses still.

"Are you OK?" Matt asked Chrissy.

"Uh... I don't know." Chrissy winced, rubbing her arm. "It's my elbow." Her blond hair was tousled from her fall, and there was a smudge of dirt on her cheek.

"Can you stand up?"

Chrissy got to her knees carefully and stood.

"What about getting back on Silver?" Matt asked. "Do you think you can ride her, if I help you get up?" She nodded a little doubtfully. Matt held his hands together for Chrissy's foot and gave her a boost. Grasping Silver's neck with her good arm, she swung her other foot over the horse's back and landed in the saddle.

"Good girl!" Matt reached up to pat Chrissy's leg. Then he untied Silver's reins and crossed them under the horse's neck before handing them to Chrissy. "This way you can control her easily. She won't be able to pull on the reins. Keep right behind me. Here's your helmet."

Ben saw how worried Susan looked. "We'll get her home and take her to the doctor, Susan. Ally wouldn't spook like Silver, he's too steady. Even if we met a nest of hornets." He laughed, but Susan didn't seem comforted.

"She's so brave!" she whispered, "I could never do that—get right back on, and with only one arm!"

Heather overheard her. "You do what you have to do," she said. " Chrissy and Silver—they know each other. And Chrissy's been off a few times. You get used to it."

Woody nodded. "You shoulda seen me bite the dust!"

Susan shuddered. Ben scowled at Woody. "Nothing's going to happen to Susan!"

Heather nodded. "Of course not. The rest of the trail is wide enough for you two to ride side by side. Woody, I'm going on ahead now. There's no cell service where we are, and I want to call the doctor. You ride back with the others." She rode past Matt and Chrissy and cantered Hendrik back to the stable, where she could use her cell phone to reach the doctor.

They all went with Chrissy to the Emergency Room. Xrays showed that her arm was broken near the elbow. After a while she came to the waiting room and showed them her arm in a white cast.

"Cool! Can we sign it?" asked Ben. They borrowed a marker from the nurse at the desk and made drawings and elaborate signatures on the cast. Matt put his name inside a rough drawing of a horse. There was a balloon coming out of the horse's mouth that read, "Come ride with me!" When Heather saw it, she wondered if Matt wanted to see more of Chrissy.

Ben drove the old pickup home, with Heather riding shotgun and Woody in the back. After they dropped him at home, the September sky began to darken. They drove on without talking through a wooded area in deep shade. Neither of them was focused on the familiar homeward road. Ben fiddled with the radio. He changed the preset button to a station that Susan liked. Heather was musing—*had Matt really kissed Chrissy when they said goodbye or only hugged her?*

Suddenly, she yelled, "Look out!"

A large moose with an enormous rack strode out of the woods into the road in front of them.

Ben braked, watching it. The pickup skidded to a halt about fifteen feet from the moose.

"Back up! Back up!" Heather was frantic.

"Why?" Ben enjoyed looking at the big animal.

"Because they're curious, and dumb, and HUGE, you idiot!"

"Well, OK."

But the moose was walking towards the pickup. His long legs covered the pavement rapidly. His nose stretched forward, sniffing at the warm motor of the pickup.

"Hurry up!" Heather held her breath.

Ben put the pickup in reverse and began to back. He turned around to look through the back window in order to stay on the road. He didn't see the moose reach the front bumper of the pickup.

"OH NO!" Heather watched the large body of the moose rise and come down on the hood! The pickup ground to a halt. There was a crunching sound. A ton of moose weight pushed the motor of the old pickup right through to the ground!

Face to face with the snout of a bull moose with a wide rack of antlers, Heather gripped Ben's shoulders and turned him around. Ben froze. Then the moose lifted his chest and front legs out of the mess he had made of the pickup and wandered off into the woods.

"Now what!?" Heather looked at Ben, grim-lipped. "That's the end of this pickup. Get out and see if we can push it off the road!"

Ben had nothing to say. He tried to put the gearshift in neutral, but there was no motor connected to it. They couldn't move the pickup with the motor dragging on the ground, so they left it where it was. Heather rolled her eyes at Ben as she took out her cell phone. At that moment a state trooper's car pulled up beside them.

"Oh, good," said Heather. "Or, not so good." She peered at the short, stout trooper who was getting out of his car.

"Had a little trouble?" inquired a voice Heather was sure she'd heard before. "Do I remember you from somewhere?"

"Maybe," Heather answered evasively. She had scolded this trooper nearly a year ago, when she had been standing over a dead deer. Now, was he going to help them, or get his own back?

She cleared her throat. "Uh, there was a moose. But he's gone now." She showed him her cell phone. "I'm just calling for help."

"Guess you don't need me then." He leered into her eyes, and Heather was sure he remembered her. She was relieved when he got back in the cruiser and took off.

Fortunately, or unfortunately, their father was home and on the way to them shortly. His only comment, when he looked at the pickup, was, "Guess the both of you'll have to figure how to buy a replacement."

He drove them home. Ben was silently counting his paychecks for the summer. No health club for him! Heather, with her hand to her mouth, had come to a different conclusion. *I'll have to sell Hendrik!*

"I know a lady who wants a Friesian." Kathy was sympathetic. "What a bummer! I'm so sorry, Heather! Wish I weren't off to college tomorrow with you feeling so low."

"He's in great shape, well-trained …" Tears were rolling down Heather's cheeks again. She rubbed them against Hendrik's neck. Perhaps the tears tickled, for he gave his great head a shake.

There was little joy in the Hobbes household. Heather hardly slept at night. Nobody talked at dinner. Heather wept into the beef stew as she stirred it. She had tissues in every pocket of her jeans. Ben was up against the hard fact that he had promised to pay for his own insurance when he got his license. Their father watched them both and said little.

Heather felt angry, frustrated, and hurt by his silence. Her mother would have taken her side! She was tired of doing everything, fixing everything, taking everything on her own back! In the mornings when she woke, she felt so weary and depressed she could hardly get out of bed. She had started courses at the nearby community college, so that she could continue to run the horse farm. Kathy was away at college, and Chrissy was travelling, so there was no girlfriend to talk to for comfort. Now she knew how it felt when Ben couldn't get moving in the morning.

A few days went by. Finally, after supper one evening, the night before Mr. Hobbes had to leave again for business, Heather came to a decision. When he sat down with his newspaper, she went to his chair and put her hand on his arm.

"Dad, please—I need to talk this thing out. It's no good crying. Ben and I have to take responsibility for what happened to the pickup. I need to know what we can do to replace it."

"I thought you'd never ask." Her father looked at her over the rims of his glasses. Heather was on tenterhooks. Ben, who was loitering within earshot, stiffened his back.

"I won't have much after I pay the insurance bill," Ben said, "but I'll hand over every pay check I ever get."

Heather nodded. "I've heard of someone who would buy Hendrik," she said, as calmly as she could. "They say I could get $12,000." She sniffed.

"You both have overlooked one thing," said their father.

Two pairs of eyebrows went up, as Heather and Ben stared at him. They waited.

"You've both forgotten that I've been paying car insurance regularly on the old pickup." He smiled at them. "Guess I could have told you sooner. Thought you needed to think about it some. It'll cost something for a safe, second-hand pickup, but the insurance will cover a lot of it."

"Wow!" Ben took a deep breath. "I thought I'd be in hock forever! How much do you reckon I'm going to owe you?"

Mr. Hobbes leaned back in his chair. "Why don't we wait to see how it adds up. For one thing, you're both hard workers. Ben, you've shown responsibility on your job while you kept up your grades this fall. And Heather—have you ever thought what I'd be paying a housekeeper to do the chores you do? Plus," he added, "you've earned a good bit with trail rides and the equine training you got Matt to do. Maybe it will all come out even."

Heather got up from the table and hugged her father. She was crying again, but this time it was from joy and love. Hendrik was hers forever!

"Kathy!" Heather ran to embrace her friend, who had returned from college to join her team-penning mates at the Farmington Fair. They hugged, as their horses waited patiently.

"Where's Chrissy?" Kathy asked.

"Here!" announced a gay voice. They turned to see Chrissy leading Silver toward them, one hand on the reins, close to the bit, the other tucked in Matt's, who walked with her. Her eyes were shining, and Heather realized with a start what a beautiful girl she was. Matt seemed to think so, too, as he pulled her toward him and, slipping his hand out from hers, slid it around her waist.

The three girls had a group hug, then Heather said firmly, "We're going in soon, and here's the strategy," she spoke in a low tone, outlining her plan. There had been no practice for weeks, while Chrissy came back from Europe, and all three were starting college, but Heather, Kathy, and Chrissy were stronger riders now, and they had last year's experience behind them.

"My dad's come!" Chrissy looked proud.

"Mine, too!" This from Kathy. Heather knew that Kathy's mother had left, giving up on life in Maine.

Matt grinned. "No one would miss this!"

"Let's go!" Heather mounted Sugar and turned her toward the arena. In her new white chaps, her white hat, and a white, fringed vest, she looked elegant. The other girls wore chaps over their jeans, too, and wide-brimmed hats over their curls. Kathy with Tess, and Chrissy on Silver followed Heather into the holding area near the arena. This time they were the last group to compete. A few men also waiting on their horses looked at them with contempt.

"Are you really goin' to try again?" one of them sneered. The three girls ignored him, as they stroked their horses necks, talking softly to them.

In the stands, Alan Hobbes and Ben sat together with Kathy's and Chrissy's fathers. They had all become acquainted over the summer. The men shook hands as they met, and so did Ben, as tall now as the other men. All four attempted to look nonchalant and confident that their girls would win.

They watched while a group of fifteen cows was brought into the arena and allowed to move freely about. Each cow had a number tied on both its sides. Then a team of three men rode their horses to the area beyond the line. A voice over a loudspeaker announced "The Riddley Boys!" The timer was alerted, and three numbers were shouted.

The three riders shot across the line and began herding cows, picking out the cows with the numbers that had been called and driving them back across the line at the other end of the arena.

The teammates whooped as they rode. There were enthusiastic shouts from the crowd. When the third cow was successfully herded across the line, the timer announced, "Three minutes and fifty seconds!" The riders looked pleased and walked their horses out of the big arena door, while the cows were being herded back to the far end of the arena.

The next team came in. They were "The Fast Draws."

"They won last year," his dad reminded Ben.

The Fast Draws were quick off the mark. All three cows they had to pen were across the line in three minutes and thirty seconds. "That'll be hard to beat, I guess," said Ben.

The next two teams were unable to match the time of three minutes, thirty seconds. Then Heather, Kathy, and Chrissy rode into the arena. There were a few cheers for them, especially from where Ben and the girls' fathers were sitting. They were the last of five teams to try for the shortest time.

Heather had been listening carefully and had memorized the numbers that had been called, so she knew which cows in the group had not been herded. She said to Kathy and Chrissy, "We're going to get 13, 9, and 2. Start looking for them now!" The numbers were hard to see, with the fifteen cows all bunched together at the end of the arena. Heather had two of them spotted when the loudspeaker announced their team as "The Lazy D riders."

As they had planned, Heather, Kathy, and Chrissy were riding toward the line when the numbers were shouted and the gong rang. Sure enough, they were 13, 9, and 2! Heather's heart was in her mouth. Could the three of them get their cows singled out quickly? She yelled, "I'm getting 13!" She kept her focus only on that cow, as she and Sugar wove their way into the small herd. Sugar lifted her small hooves neatly, dodging left and right, following Heather's signals as they cut the cow from the huddled herd and nudged her back towards the line. She hoped Kathy and Chrissy were doing the same with numbers 2 and 9. Looking over her shoulder, she saw them almost abreast of her. Kathy's hat was hanging around her neck, but her grip was firm on the reins, and she and Tess were herding cow No.2 expertly. Chrissy flew across the arena on Silver, driving cow No.9 before her. At almost the same time the three cows passed the line.

The timer announced with excitement, "Ladies and gentlemen, you're not going to believe this! The time on this was just under three minutes!"

The stadium went wild with cheers and whoops and whistles. Heather looked toward her father in the stands. He was waving his arms wildly, and, in the next row, a tall, red-headed young man was throwing his baseball cap in the air. Russ! He had made it here from veterinary school, after all! Her cheeks pink, Heather rode out with Kathy and Chrissy to accept the team penning prize—three hundred dollars! Cameras flashed as reporters recorded the event. Alan Hobbes and Ben could hardly get through the applauding crowd to congratulate Heather and take pictures of the three girls holding their horses.

They found Chrissy hugging Matt, and Heather hugging Russ. "Just saying 'Hi'," Heather said sheepishly. She introduced Russ to her father and looked around for Kathy. To her surprise, Kathy was walking toward them, arm-in-arm with a good-looking young man with dark hair.

"Ted's a friend from college," Kathy said airily, as she named her companions for him. "He has an Arabian!"

"Wow!" There was general excitement and hugs and promises to get together during Thanksgiving break.

On the way home in the car, Heather said to her dad, "Were those other men ever surprised! They sneered at us and made jokes before we started. But they didn't have much to say afterwards!"

It was a late fall evening. A few deer were nibbling at corn stalks in the field garden behind the barn. Heather rode out of a trail on Hendrik and turned him toward the barn. As they crossed in front of it, a bright, red pickup came up the drive. She saw Ben in the driver's seat, a smile on his face. She no longer worried about his running into trouble. A year had made a difference in his good sense, as well as his size.

Ben gunned the motor as he swung into a spot near them and braked hard. "This truck has great springs," he announced cheerily. "Remember how creaky and jolty the old one was?"

"Please." Heather slid her feet out of the stirrups, rolled off Hendrik, and slid three feet to the ground. "I don't want to think about that old wreck. Or that moose!" she added, leading Hendrik into the barn. He went smoothly, not bothered anymore by the motor of the pickup, parked so nearby. Heather used it now to commute to the nearby community college where she worked toward a degree while maintaining the horse farm. And her younger brother!

Ben got out of the new pickup and stood back, admiring its color and dent-free surface. "You can use it for your Christmas Ball," he offered airily. "Russ can drive you. He's taking you, isn't he?"

"Probably. Or perhaps. It's still two months away."

"Come to think of it, he'll probably pick you up with a limo!" Ben was pleased to see Heather blush. "Wouldn't that put Matt's nose out of joint!"

"Matt's got another interest." Heather thought about seeing him with his arms around Chrissy on the day they won the team-penning contest. Chrissy looked happy, and Heather was glad. She had good memories herself, like a certain kiss when she and Russ got back after the Equine Fair.

"He doesn't know a terrific interest when he sees one!" Ben was tall enough to hang his arm around Heather's shoulder, as they walked toward the farmhouse. When they opened the door, a small, fat pig hurtled toward them, demanding his supper.

Heather's cell phone chimed. She checked the number and put the phone to her ear. "Hi Russ ... Sure! I'd love to!" She cocked an eyebrow at Ben.

Outside, the air felt crisp and smelled of apples. From the sky, a few snowflakes floated down. The deer went on munching as it grew dark.

About the Author

MOLLIE SCHMIDT IS A retired psychologist who has published two children's books, "Willem of Holland," and "Levi." She is a member of SCBWI and has a website at www.mollieschmidt. com. Her poetry and reviews have appeared in various anthologies and journals. She lives in Central Maine near many horse farms and loves to tell stories about them.